"What do you want from me? I will not and could not love a woman like you!"

"Oh, that honesty...hits me right where it hurts," Maxie trilled, a knife-like pain scything through her. "But for all that, you still want me, don't you? Do you know something, Angelos? I *like* knowing that."

Those stunning black eyes burned with rage and seething pride. "So, quote me a price for one night in your bed. What do you think you would be worth?"

The derisive suggestion coiled like a whip around her and scared her worse than a beating. "You couldn't even make the bidding.... You see, I learn from my mistakes, Angelos. The next man I live with will be my husband...."

Dear Reader,

What I enjoy most about writing is the creation of entirely different heroines. THE HUSBAND HUNTERS is about three women who find love where they least expect it. Maxie cannot imagine any man appreciating her for herself, rather than her looks. Darcy had been badly hurt and has given up on the male sex. Polly falls in love and is betrayed. To match these ladies, we have Angelos, who fondly imagines that Maxie will be his the instant he asks; Luca, who seeks revenge by ensuring that Darcy marries no one but him; and Raul, who finds out the hard way that Polly, the idealistic mother of his child, can be surprisingly unforgiving....

Sincerely,

Lynne Graham

Look out next month for Darcy's story:
The Vengeful Husband by Lynne Graham
Harlequin Presents® #2007

LYNNE GRAHAM

Married to a Mistress

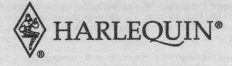

TORONTO • NEW YORK • LONDON
AMSTERDAM • PARIS • SYDNEY • HAMBURG
STOCKHOLM • ATHENS • TOKYO • MILAN • MADRID
PRAGUE • WARSAW • BUDAPEST • AUCKLAND

ISBN 0-373-12001-X

MARRIED TO A MISTRESS

First North American Publication 1999.

CHAPTER ONE

'AND since Leland has given me power of attorney over his affairs, I shall trail that little tramp through the courts and *ruin* her!' Jennifer Coulter announced with vindictive satisfaction.

Angelos Petronides surveyed his late mother's English stepsister with no more than polite attention, his distaste concealed, his brilliant black eyes expressionless. Nobody would ever have guessed that within the last sixty seconds Jennifer had made his day by putting him in possession of information he would've paid a considerable amount to gain. Maxie Kendall, the model dubbed the Ice Queen by the press, the one and only woman who had ever given Angelos a sleepless night, was in debt...

'Leland spent a fortune on her too!' As she stalked his vast and impressive London office, Jennifer exuded seething resentment. 'You should see the bills I've uncovered...you wouldn't *believe* what it cost to keep that little trollop in designer clothes!'

'A mistress expects a decent wardrobe...and Maxie Kendall is ambitious. I imagine she took Leland for everything she could get.' Angelos stoked the flames of his visitor's outrage without a flicker of conscience.

Unlike most who had witnessed the breakup of the Coulter marriage three years earlier, he had never suffered from the misapprehension that Leland had deserted a whiter than white wife. Nor was he impressed by Jennifer's pleas of penury. The middle-aged blonde had been born wealthy and would die even wealthier, and her miserly habits were a frequent source of malicious amusement in London society.

'All that money gone for good,' Jennifer recounted tight-mouthed. 'And *now* I find out that the little tart got this huge loan off Leland as well—'

Imperceptibly, Angelos had tensed again. Trollop, tart? Jennifer had no class, no discretion. A mistress was a ne-cessity to a red-blooded male, but a whore wasn't. However, Leland *had* broken the rules. An intelligent man did not leave his wife to set up home with his mistress. No Greek male would ever have been that stupid, Angelos re-flected with innate superiority. Leland Coulter had made a fool of himself and he had embarrassed his entire family.

'But you have regained what you said you wanted most,' he slotted into the flood of Jennifer's financial recrimina-tions. 'You have your husband back.'

The dry reminder made the older woman flush and then her mouth twisted again. 'Oh, yes, I got him back after his heart attack, so weak he's going to be recuperating for months! That bitch deserted him at the hospital...did I tell you that? Simply told the doctor to contact his wife and walked back out again, cool as a cucumber. Well, I *need* that money now, and whatever it takes I intend to get it off her. I've already had a lawyer's letter sent to her—'

'Jennifer...with Leland laid low, you have many more important concerns. And I assure you that Leland would not be impressed by the spectacle of his wife driving his former mistress into the bankruptcy court.' From below lush black lashes, Angelos watched the blonde stiffen as she belatedly considered that angle. 'Allow *me* to deal with this matter. I will assume responsibility for the loan and reimburse you.'

Jennifer's jaw slackened in shock. 'You...you *will*?'

'Are we not family?' Angelos chided in his deep, dark, accented drawl.

Slowly, very slowly, Jennifer nodded, fascinated against her will. Those incredible black eyes looked almost warm, and since warmth was not a character trait she had ever

associated with Angelos Petronides before she was thrown
off balance.

The head of the Petronides clan, and regarded with immense respect by every member, Angelos was ruthless, remorseless and coldly self-sufficient. He was also fabulously
wealthy, flamboyantly unpredictable and frighteningly
powerful. He scared people; he scared people just by strolling into a room. When Leland had walked out on his marriage, Angelos had silenced Jennifer's martyred sobs with
one sardonic and deeply unsympathetic glance. Somehow
Angelos had discovered that *her* infidelity had come first.
Chagrined by that galling awareness, Jennifer had avoided
him ever since...

Only the greater fear of what might happen to Leland's
international chain of highly profitable casinos under her
own inexpert guidance had driven her to approach Angelos
for practical advice and assistance. Indeed, just at the moment Jennifer could not quite comprehend *how* she had
been led into revealing her plans to destroy Maxie Kendall.

'You'll make her pay...?' Jennifer prompted dry-
mouthed.

'My methods are my own,' Angelos murmured without
apology, making it clear that the matter of the loan was no
longer her province.

That hard, strikingly handsome face wore an expression
that now chilled Jennifer. But she was triumphant. Clearly
family ties, even distant ones, meant more to Angelos than
she had ever dreamt. That little trollop would suffer; that
was *all* Jennifer wanted.

When he was alone again, Angelos did something he had
never been known to do before. He shattered his secretary
by telling her to hold all his calls. He lounged indolently
back in his leather chair in apparent contemplation of the
panoramic view of the City of London. But his eyes were
distant. No more cold showers. A sensual smile slowly
formed on his well-shaped mouth. No more lonely nights.
His smile flashed to unholy brilliance. The Ice Queen was

his. After a three-year-long waiting game, she was finally to become *his*.

Mercenary and outwardly cold as she was…exquisite, though, indeed so breathtakingly beautiful that even Angelos, jaded and often bored connoisseur that he considered himself to be, had been stunned the first time he saw Maxie Kendall in the flesh. She looked like the Sleeping Beauty of popular fable. Untouchable, *untouched*… A grim laugh escaped Angelos. What nonsensical imagery the mind could serve up! She had been the mistress of a man old enough to be her grandfather for the past three years. There was nothing remotely innocent about the lady.

But for all that he would not use the loan like a battering ram. He would be a gentleman. He would be subtle. He would rescue her from her monetary embarrassments, earn her gratitude and ultimately inspire her loyalty as Leland had never contrived to do. She would not be cold with *him*. And, in reward, he would cocoon her in luxury, set the jewel of her perfection to a fitting frame and fulfil her every want and need. She would never have to work again. What more could any rational woman want?

Blissfully unaware of the detailed plans being formed on her behalf, Maxie climbed out of the cab she had caught from the train station. Every movement fluid with long-limbed natural grace, her spectacular trademark mane of golden hair blowing in the breeze, she straightened to her full five feet eleven inches and stared at her late godmother's home. Gilbourne was an elegant Georgian house set in wonderful grounds.

As she approached the front door her heart ached and she blinked back tears. The day she had made her first public appearance in Leland's company, her godmother, Nancy Leeward, had written to tell her that she would no longer be a welcome visitor here. But four months ago her godmother had come to see her in London. There had been a reconciliation of sorts, only Nancy hadn't said she was ill, hadn't given so much as a hint—nor had Maxie received word of her death until *after* the funeral.

So somehow it seemed all wrong to be showing up now for a reading of Nancy's last will and testament...and, worst of all, to be nourishing desperate prayers that at the last her godmother had somehow found it within her heart to forgive her for a lifestyle she had deemed scandalous.

In her slim envelope bag Maxie already carried a letter which had blown her every hope of future freedom to smithereens. It had arrived only that morning. And it had reminded her of a debt she had naively assumed would be written off when Leland severed their relationship and let her go. He had already taken three irreplaceable years of her life, and she had poured every penny she earned as a model into repaying what she could of that loan.

Hadn't that been enough to satisfy him? Right now she was homeless and broke and lurid publicity had severely curtailed her employment prospects. Leland had been vain and monumentally self-centred but he had never been cruel and he was certainly not poor. Why was he doing this to her? Couldn't he even have given her time to get back on her feet again before pressing her for payment?

The housekeeper answered the door before Maxie could reach for the bellpush. Her plump face was stiff with disapproval. 'Miss Kendall.' It was the coldest of welcomes. 'Miss Johnson and Miss Fielding are waiting in the drawing-room. Mrs Leeward's solicitor, Mr Hartley, should be here soon.'

'Thank you...no, there's no need to show me the way; I remember it well.'

Within several feet of the drawing-room, however, not yet ready to face the other two women and frankly nervous of the reception she might receive from one of them, Maxie paused at the window which overlooked the rose garden that had been Nancy Leeward's pride and joy. Her memory slid back to hazily recalled summer afternoon tea parties for three little girls. Maxine, Darcy and Polly, each of them on their very best behaviour for Nancy, who had never had a child of her own, had had pre-war values and expectations of her goddaughters.

Of the three, Maxie had always been the odd one out. Both Darcy and Polly came from comfortable backgrounds. They had always been smartly dressed when they came to stay at Gilbourne but Maxie had never had anything decent to wear, and every year, without fail, Nancy had taken Maxie shopping for clothes. How shocked her godmother would've been had she ever learned that Maxie's father had usually sold those expensive garments the minute his daughter got home again...

Her late mother, Gwen, had once been Nancy's companion—a paid employee but for all that Nancy had always talked of her as a friend. Her godmother, however, had thoroughly disliked the man her companion and friend had chosen to marry.

Weak, selfish, unreliable... Russ Kendall was, unfortunately, all of those things, but he was also the only parent Maxie had ever known and Maxie was loyal. Her father had brought her up alone, loving her to the best of his ability. That she had never been able to trust him to behave himself around a woman as wealthy as Nancy Leeward had just been a cross Maxie had had to bear.

Every time Russ Kendall had brought his daughter to Gilbourne to visit he had overstayed his welcome, striving to butter her godmother up with compliments before trying to borrow money from her, impervious to the chill of the older woman's distaste. Maxie had always been filled with guilty relief when her father departed again. Only then had she been able to relax and enjoy herself.

'I thought I heard a car but I must've been mistaken. I wish Maxie would come...I'm looking forward to seeing her again,' a female voice said quite clearly.

Maxie twisted in surprise to survey the drawing-room door, only now registering that it was ajar. That had been Polly's voice, soft and gentle, just like Polly herself.

'That's one thrill I could live without,' a second female voice responded tartly. 'Maxie, the living doll—'

'She can't help being beautiful, Darcy.'

Outside the door, Maxie had frozen, unnerved by the biting hostility she had heard in Darcy's cuttingly well-bred voice. So Darcy *still* hadn't managed to forgive her, and yet what had destroyed their friendship three years earlier had been in no way Maxie's fault. Darcy had been jilted at the altar. Her bridegroom had waited until the eleventh hour to confess that he had fallen in love with one of her bridesmaids. That bridesmaid, entirely innocent of the smallest instant of flirtation *with* or indeed interest *in* the bridegroom, had unfortunately been Maxie.

'Does that somehow excuse her for stealing someone else's husband?'

'I don't think any of us get to choose *who* we fall in love with,' Polly stressed with a surprising amount of emotion. 'And Maxie must be devastated now that he's gone back to his wife.'

'If Maxie ever falls in love, it won't be with an ancient old bloke like that,' Darcy scorned. 'She wouldn't have looked twice at Leland Coulter if he hadn't been loaded! Surely you haven't forgotten what her father was like? Greed is in Maxie's bloodstream. Don't you remember the way Russ was always trying to touch poor Nancy for a loan?'

'I remember how much his behaviour embarrassed and upset Maxie,' Polly responded tautly, her dismay at the other woman's attitude audible.

In the awful pool of silence that followed Maxie wrapped her arms round herself. She felt gutted, totally gutted. So nothing had changed. Darcy was stubborn and never admitted herself in the wrong. Maxie had, however, hoped that time would've lessened the other woman's antagonism to the point where they could at least make peace.

'She *is* stunningly beautiful. Who can really blame her for taking advantage of that?' Darcy breathed in a grudging effort at placation. 'But then what else has Maxie got? I never did think she had much in the way of brains—'

'How can you say that, Darcy? Maxie is severely dyslexic,' Polly reminded her companion reproachfully.

Maxie lost all her natural colour, cringing at even this whispered reference to her biggest secret.

The tense silence in the drawing-room lingered.

'And in spite of that she's so wonderfully famous now,' Polly sighed.

'Well, if your idea of fame is playing Goldilocks in shampoo commercials, I suppose she is,' Darcy shot back crushingly.

Unfreezing, Maxie tiptoed back down the corridor and then walked with brisk, firm steps back again. She pushed wide the door with a light smile pasted to her unwittingly pale face.

'Maxie!' Polly carolled, and rose rather awkwardly to her feet.

Halfway towards her, Maxie stopped dead. Tiny dark-haired Polly was pregnant.

'When did you get married?' Maxie demanded with a grin.

Polly turned brick-red. 'I didn't…I mean, I'm *not*…'

Maxie was stunned. Polly had been raised by a fire-breathing puritanical father. The teenager Maxie recalled had been wonderfully kind and caring, but also extremely prim and proper as a result. Horribly aware that she had embarrassed Polly, she forced a laugh. 'So what?' she said lightly.

'I'm afraid the event of a child without a husband is not something as easily shrugged off in Polly's world as in yours.' Darcy stood by the window, her boyishly short auburn hair catching fire from the light behind her, aggressive green eyes challenging on the point.

Maxie stiffened at the reminder that Darcy had a child of her own but she refused to rise to that bait. Poor Polly looked strained enough as it was. 'Polly knows what I meant—'

'Does she—?' Darcy began.

'I feel dizzy!' Polly announced with startling abruptness.

Instantly Darcy stopped glaring at Maxie and both women anxiously converged on the tiny brunette. Maxie was the more efficient helper. Gently easing Polly down into the nearest armchair, she fetched a footstool because the smaller woman's ankles looked painfully swollen. Then, noting the untouched tea trolley nearby, she poured Polly a cup of tea and urged her to eat a digestive biscuit.

'Do you think you should see a doctor?' Darcy asked ruefully. 'I suppose I was lucky. I was never ill when I was expecting Zia.'

'What do you think, Polly?' Maxie prompted.

'I'm fine…saw one yesterday,' Polly muttered. 'I'm just tired.'

At that point, a middle-aged man in a dark suit was shown in with great ceremony by the housekeeper. Introducing himself as Edward Hartley, their godmother's solicitor, he took a seat, politely turned down the offer of refreshment and briskly extracted a document from his briefcase.

'Before I commence the reading of the will, I feel that I should warn you all beforehand that the respective monies will only be advanced *if* the strict conditions laid down by my late client are met—'

'Put that in English,' Darcy interrupted impatiently.

Mr Hartley removed his spectacles with a faint sigh. 'I assume that you are all aware that Mrs Leeward enjoyed a very happy but tragically brief marriage when she was in her twenties, and that the premature death of her husband was a lifelong source of sorrow and regret to her.'

'Yes,' Polly confirmed warmly. 'Our godmother often talked to us about Robbie.'

'He died in a car crash six months after they married,' Maxie continued ruefully. 'As time went on he became pretty much a saint in her memory. She used to talk to us about marriage as if it was some kind of Holy Grail and a woman's only hope of happiness.'

'Before her death, Mrs Leeward made it her business to visit each one of you. After completing those visits, she altered her will,' Edward Hartley informed them in a tone of wry regret. 'I advised her that the conditions of inheritance she chose to include might be very difficult, if not impossible for any one of you to fulfil. However, Mrs Leeward was a lady who knew her own mind, and she had made her decision.'

Maxie was holding her breath, her bemused gaze skimming over the faces of her companions. Polly wore an expression of blank exhaustion but Darcy, never able to hide her feelings, now looked worried sick.

In the pin-dropping silence, the solicitor began to read the will. Nancy Leeward had left her entire and extremely substantial estate evenly divided between her three goddaughters on condition that each of them married within a year and remained married for a minimum of six months. Only then would they qualify to inherit a portion of the estate. In the event of any one of them failing to meet the terms of the will, that person's share would revert to the Crown.

By the time the older man had finished speaking, Maxie was in shock. Every scrap of colour had drained from her face. She had hoped, she had *prayed* that she might be released from the burden of debt that had almost destroyed her life. And now she had learnt that, like everything else over the past twenty-two years, from the death of her mother when she was a toddler to her father's compulsive gambling addiction, nothing was going to be that easy.

A jagged laugh broke from Darcy. 'You've just got to be kidding,' she said incredulously.

'There's no chance of me fulfilling those conditions,' Polly confided chokily, glancing at her swollen stomach and looking away again with open embarrassment.

'Nor I...' Maxie admitted flatly, her attention resting on Polly and her heart sinking for her. She should have guessed there would be no supportive male in the picture. Trusting, sweet-natured Polly had obviously been seduced and dumped.

Darcy shot Maxie an exasperated look. 'They'll be queuing up for you, Maxie—'

'With my colourful reputation?'

Darcy flushed. 'All any one of us requires is a man and a wedding ring. Personally speaking, I'll only attract either by advertising and offering a share of the proceeds as a bribe!'

'While I am sure that that is a purely facetious comment, made, as it were, in the heat of the moment, I must point out that the discovery of any such artificial arrangement would automatically disqualify you from inheriting any part of your godmother's estate,' Edward Hartley asserted with extreme gravity.

'You may say our godmother knew her own mind...but I *think*...well, I'd better not say what I think,' Darcy gritted, respect for a much loved godmother evidently haltering her abrasive tongue.

Simultaneously, a shaken little laugh of reluctant appreciation was dredged from Maxie. *She* was not in the dark. The reasoning behind Nancy Leeward's will was as clear as daylight to her. Within recent months their godmother had visited each one of them...and what a severe disappointment they must all have been.

She had found Maxie apparently living in sin with an older married man. She had discovered that Polly was well on the road to becoming an unmarried mother. And Darcy? Maxie's stomach twisted with guilt. Some months after that day of cruel humiliation in the church, Darcy had given birth to a baby. Was it any wonder that the redhead had been a vehement man-hater ever since?

'It's such a shame that your godmother tied her estate up like that,' Maxie's friend, Liz, lamented the following afternoon as the two women discussed the solicitor's letter which had bluntly demanded the immediate settlement of Leland Coulter's loan. 'If she hadn't, all your problems would've been solved.'

'Maybe I should have told Nancy the real reason why I was living in Leland's house...but I couldn't have stood her thinking that I was expecting *her* to buy me out of trouble. It wouldn't have been fair to put her in that position either. She really did detest my father.' Maxie gave a fatalistic shrug. She had suffered too many disappointments in life to waste time crying over spilt milk.

'Well, what you need now is some good legal advice. You were only nineteen when you signed that loan agreement and you were under tremendous pressure. You were genuinely afraid for your father's life.' Liz's freckled face below her mop of greying sandy hair looked hopeful. 'Surely that *has* to make a difference?'

From the other side of the kitchen table, casually clad in faded jeans and a loose shirt, Maxie studied the friend who had without question taken her in off the street and freely offered her a bed for as long as she needed it. Liz Blake was the only person she trusted with her secrets. Liz, bless her heart, had never been influenced by the looks that so often made other women hostile or uneasy in Maxie's company. Blind from birth and fiercely independent, Liz made a comfortable living as a potter and enjoyed a wide and varied social circle.

'I signed what I signed and it did get Dad off the hook,' Maxie reminded her.

'Some thanks you got for your sacrifice.'

'Dad's never asked me for money since—'

'Maxie...you haven't *seen* him for three years,' Liz pointed out grimly.

Maxie tensed. 'Because he's ashamed, Liz. He feels guilty around me now.'

Liz frowned as her guide dog, Bounce, a glossy black

Labrador, sprang up and nudged his head against her knee.
'I wonder who that is coming to the door. I'm not expecting
anyone…and nobody outside the mail redirection service
and that modelling agency of yours is supposed to know
you're here!'

By the time the doorbell actually went, Liz was already
in the hall moving to answer it. A couple of minutes later
she reappeared in the doorway. 'You have a visitor…foreign, male, very tall, very attractive voice. He also
says he's a very good friend of yours—'

'Of mine?' Maxie queried with a perplexed frown.

Liz shook her head. 'He *has* to be a good friend to have
worked out where you're hiding out. And Bounce gave him
the all-over suspicious sniff routine and passed him with
honours so I put him in the lounge. Look, I'll be in the
studio, Maxie. I need to finish off that order before I leave
tomorrow.'

Maxie wondered who on earth had managed to find her.
The press? Oh, dear heaven, had Liz trustingly invited some
sneaky journalist in? Taut with tension, she hurried down
the hall into the lounge.

One step into that small cosy room, she stopped dead as
if she had run into a brick wall without warning. Smash,
crash, her mind screamed as she took a sudden instinctive
backward step, shock engulfing her in rolling waves of dis-
orientation.

'Maxie…how are you?' Angelos Petronides purred as he
calmly extended a lean brown hand in conventional greeting.

Maxie gaped as if a boa constrictor had risen in front of
her, her heart thumping at manic speed and banging in her
eardrums. A very good friend. Had Liz misheard him?

'Mr Petronides—?'

'Angelos, please,' he countered with a very slight smile.

Maxie blinked. She had never seen him smile before. She
had been in this arrogant male's company half a dozen
times over the past three years and this was the very first

time he had deigned to verbally acknowledge that she lived and breathed. In her presence he had talked around her as if she wasn't there, switching to Greek if she made any attempt to enter the conversation, and on three separate occasions, evidently responding to his request, Leland had sent her home early in a taxi.

With rock-solid assurance, Angelos let his hand drop again. Amusement at her stupefied state flashed openly in his brilliant black eyes.

Maxie stiffened. 'I'm afraid I can't imagine what could bring you here…or indeed how you found me—'

'Were you ever lost?' Angelos enquired with husky innuendo while he ran heavily lidded heated dark eyes over her lithe, slender frame with extraordinarily insulting thoroughness. 'I suspect that you know very well why I am here.'

Her fair skin burning, Maxie's sapphire blue eyes shuttered. 'I haven't the slightest idea—'

'You are now a free woman.'

This is not happening to me, a little voice screeched in the back of Maxie's mind. She folded her arms, saw those terrifyingly shrewd eyes read her defensive body language and lowered her arms again, fighting not to coil her straining fingers into fists.

One unguarded moment almost six months ago… Was that all it had taken to encourage him? He had caught her watching him and instantaneously, as if that momentary abstraction of hers had been a blatant invitation, he had reacted with a lightning flash look of primitive male sexual hunger. A split second later he had turned away again, but that shatteringly unexpected response of his had shaken Maxie inside out.

She had told herself she had imagined it. She had almost cherished this arrogant Greek tycoon's indifference to her as a woman. OK, so possibly, once or twice, his ability to behave as if she was invisible had irritated and humiliated her, but then she had seen some excuse for his behaviour.

Unlike Leland, Angelos Petronides would never be guilty of a need to show off a woman like a prize poodle at what was supposed to be a business meeting.

'And now that you *are* free, I want you in my life,' Angelos informed her with the supreme confident cool of a male who had never been refused anything he wanted by a woman. Not a male primed for rejection, not a male who had even contemplated that as a remote possibility. His attitude spoke volumes for his opinion of her morals.

And at that mortifying awareness Maxie trembled, her usual deadpan, wonderful and absolute control beginning to fray round the edges. 'You really believe that you can just walk in here and *tell* me——?'

'Yes,' Angelos cut in with measured impatience. 'Don't be coy. You have no need to play such games with me. I have not been unaware of your interest in me.'

Her very knees wobbled with rage, a rage such as Maxie had never known before. He had the subtlety of a sledgehammer, the blazing self-image of a sun god. The very first time she had seen Angelos Petronides she *had* had a struggle to stop staring. Lethally attractive men were few and far between; fiercely intelligent and lethally attractive men were even fewer. And the natural brute power Angelos radiated like an aura of intimidation executed its own fatal fascination.

He had filled her with intense curiosity but that was *all*. Maxie had never learnt what it was like to actually want a man. She didn't like most men; she didn't trust them. What man had ever seen her as an individual with emotions and thoughts that might be worth a moment's attention? What man had ever seen her as anything more than a glamorous one-dimensional trophy to hang on his arm and boast about?

As a teenager, Maxie had always been disillusioned, angered or frankly repelled long before she could reach the stage of reciprocating male interest. And now Angelos Petronides had just proved himself the same as the rest of the common herd. What she couldn't understand was why she should be feeling a fierce, embittered stab of stark disappointment.

'You're trembling…why don't you sit down?' Angelos switched into full domineering mode with the polished ease of a duck taking to water and drew up an armchair for her occupancy. When she failed to move, the black eyes beneath those utterly enviable long inky lashes rested on her in irritated reproof. 'You have shadows under your eyes. You have lost weight. You should be taking better care of yourself.'

She would *not* lose her temper; she would tie herself in knots before she exposed her outrage and he recognised her humiliation. How dared he…how *dared* he land on Liz's doorstep and announce his lustful intentions and behave as if he was awaiting a round of applause? If she spread herself across the carpet at his feet in gratitude, he would no doubt happily take it in his stride.

'Your interest in my wellbeing is unwelcome and unnecessary, Mr Petronides,' Maxie countered not quite levelly, and she sat down because she was honestly afraid that if she didn't she might give way to temptation and slap him across that insolent mouth so hard she would bruise her fingers.

He sank down opposite her, which was an instant relief because even when she was standing he towered over her. That was an unusual sensation for a woman as tall as Maxie, and one that with him in the starring role she found irrationally belittling.

For such a big, powerfully built man, however, he moved with the lightness and ease of an athlete. He was as dark as she was fair…quite staggeringly good-looking. Spectacular cheekbones, a strong, thin-bladed nose, the wide mouth of a sensualist. But it was those extraordinary eyes which held and compelled and lent such blazing definition to his fantastic bone structure. And there was not a soupçon of softness or real emotion in that hard, assessing gaze.

'Leland's wife was planning to take you to court over that loan,' Angelos Petronides delivered smoothly into the thumping silence.

Maxie's spine jerked rigid, eyes flying wide in shock as she gasped, 'How did you find out about the loan?'

Angelos angled a broad, muscular shoulder in a light, dismissive shrug, as if they were enjoying a light and casual conversation. 'It's not important. Jennifer will *not* take you to court. I have settled the loan on your behalf.'

Slowly, her muscles strangely unwilling to do her bidding, Maxie leant forward. 'Say that again,' she invited shakily, because she couldn't believe he had said what he had just said.

Angelos Petronides regarded her with glittering black unfathomable eyes. 'I will not hold that debt over you, Maxie. My intervention was a gesture of good faith alone.'

'G-good *faith*...?' Maxie stammered helplessly, her voice rising to shrillness in spite of her every effort to control it.

'What else could it be?' Angelos shifted a graceful hand in eloquent emphasis, his brilliant gaze absorbing the raw incredulity and shock which had blown a giant smoking crater in the Ice Queen's famed façade of cool. 'What man worthy of the name would seek to blackmail a woman into his bed?'

CHAPTER TWO

MAXIE leapt upright, her beautiful face a flushed mask of fury. 'Do you think I am a complete fool?' she shouted at him so loudly her voice cracked.

Unhurriedly, Angelos Petronides shifted his incredibly long legs and fluidly unfolded to his full height again, his complete control mocking her loss of temper. 'With regard to some of your past decisions in life...how frank am I allowed to be?'

Maxie sucked in oxygen as if she was drowning, clamped a hand to her already opening mouth and spun at speed away from him. She was shattered that he had smashed her self-discipline. As noise filtered through the open window she became dimly aware of the shouts of children playing football somewhere outside, but their voices were like sounds impinging from another world.

'You don't need to apologise,' Angelos drawled in a mocking undertone. 'I've seen your temper many times before. You go pale and you stiffen. Every time Leland put so much as a finger on you in public, I witnessed your struggle not to shrug him off. It must have been fun in the bedroom...'

Maxie's slender backbone quivered. Her fingernails flexed like claws longing to make contact with human flesh. She wanted to *kill* him. But she couldn't even trust herself to speak, and was all the more agitated by the simple fact that she had never felt such rage before and honestly didn't know how to cope with it.

'But then, it was always evident to me that Leland's biggest thrill was trotting you out in public at every possible opportunity. ''Look at me, I have a blonde twice as tall as me and a third of my age,''' Angelos mused with earthy amusement. 'I suspect he might not have demanded intimate entertainment that often. He wasn't a young man...'

'And you are...without doubt...the most offensive, objectionable man I have ever met!' Maxie launched with her back still rigidly turned to him.

'I am a taste you will acquire. After all, you *need* someone like me.' A pair of strong hands settled without warning on her slim shoulders and exerted sufficient pressure to swivel her back round to face him.

'I need someone like you like I need a hole in the head!' Maxie railed back at him rawly as she tore herself free of that controlling hold. 'And keep your hands off me...I don't like being pawed!'

'Why are you so angry? I *had* to tell you about the loan,' Angelos pointed out calmly. 'I was aware that the Coulters' lawyer had already been in touch. Naturally, I wanted to set your mind at rest.'

The reminder of the debt that had simply been transferred acted like a drenching flood of cold water on Maxie's overheated emotions. Her angry flush was replaced by waxen pallor. Her body turned cold and weak and shaky and she studied the worn carpet at his feet. 'You've bought yourself a pup. I can't settle that loan...and right now I haven't even got enough to make a payment on it,' she framed sickly.

'Why do you get yourself so worked up about nothing?' Angelos released an extravagant sigh. 'Sit down before you fall down. Haven't I already given you my assurance that I have no intention of holding that former debt over your head in any way? But, in passing, may I ask what you needed that loan for?'

'I got into a real financial mess, that's all,' she muttered evasively, protecting her father as she always did, conscious of the derisive distaste such weakness roused in other, stronger men. And, drained by her outbursts and ashamed of them, she found herself settling back down into the chair again.

For the very first time she was genuinely scared of Angelos Petronides. He owned a piece of her, just as Leland once had, but he would be expecting infinitely more than a charade in return. She wasn't taken in by his reassurances, or by that roughly gentle intonation she had never dreamt he might possess. In the space of ten minutes he had reduced her to a babbling, screeching wreck and, for now, he was merely content to have made his domineering presence felt.

'Money is not a subject I discuss with women,' Angelos told her quietly. 'It is most definitely not a subject I ever wish to discuss with you again.'

Angelos Petronides, billionaire and benevolence personified? Maxie shuddered with disbelief. Did he ever read his own publicity? She had sat in on business meetings chaired by him, truly unforgettable experiences. The King and his terrified minions, who behaved as if at any moment he might snap and shout, 'Off with their heads!' Grown men perspired and stammered with nerves in his presence, cowered when he shot down their suggestions, went into cold panic if he frowned. He did not suffer fools gladly.

He had a brilliant mind, but that superior intellect had made him inherently devious and manipulative. He controlled the people around him. In comparison, Leland Coulter had been harmless. Maxie had *coped* with Leland. And Leland, give him his due, had never tried to pose as her only friend in a hostile world. But over her now loomed a six-foot-four-inch giant threat without a conscience.

'I know where you're coming from,' Maxie heard herself admit out loud as she lifted her beautiful head again.

Angelos gazed down at her with steady black eyes. 'Then why all the histrionics?'

Maxie gulped, disconcerted to feel that awful surge of temper rise again. With that admission she had expected to make him wary, force him to ease back. About the last reaction she had expected was his cool acknowledgement that she was intelligent enough to recognise his tactics for what they were. The iron hand in the velvet glove.

'Have dinner with me tonight,' Angelos suggested smoothly. 'We can talk then. You need some time to think things over.'

'I need no time whatsoever.' Maxie stared back up into those astonishingly dark and impenetrable eyes and suffered the oddest light-headed sensation, as if the floor had shifted beneath her. Her lashes fluttered, a slight bemused frown line drawing her fine brows together as she shook her head slightly, long golden hair thick as skein on skein of silk rippling round her shoulders. 'I will not be your mistress.'

'I haven't asked yet.'

A cynical laugh was torn from Maxie as she rose restively to her feet again. 'You don't need to be that specific. I certainly didn't imagine you were planning to offer me anything more respectable. And, no, I do *not* intend to discuss this any further,' she asserted tightly, carefully focusing on a point to the left of him, the tip of her tongue stealing out to moisten her dry lower lip in a swift defensive motion. 'So either you are a good loser or a bad loser, Mr Petronides...I imagine I'll find out which soon enough—'

'I do not lose,' Angelos breathed in a roughened undertone. 'I am also very persistent. If you make yourself a challenge, I will resent the waste of time demanded by pursuit but, like any red-blooded male, I will undoubtedly want you even more.'

Without even knowing why, Maxie shivered. There was the most curious buzz in the atmosphere, sending tiny little warning pulses of alarm through her tautening length. Her unsettled and bemused eyes swerved involuntarily back to him and locked into the ferocious hold of his compelling scrutiny.

'I will also become angry with you,' Angelos forecast, shifting soundlessly closer, his husky drawl thickening and lowering in pitch to a mesmeric level of intimacy. 'You made Leland jump through no hoops...why should I? And I would treat you *so* much better than he did. I know what a woman likes. I know what makes a woman of your nature feel secure and appreciated, what makes her happy, content, *satisfied...*'

Like a child drawn too close to a blazing fire in spite of all warnings, Maxie was transfixed. She could feel her own heartbeat accelerating, the blood surging rich and vibrantly alive through her veins. A kind of craving, an almost ter-rifying upswell of excitement potently and powerfully new to her gripped her.

'A-Angelos...?' she whispered, feeling dizzy and disori-entated.

He reached out and drew her to him without once break-ing that spellbinding appraisal. 'How easily you can say my name...'

And she said it again, like a supplicant eager to please.

Those stunning eyes of his blazed gold as a hot sun with satisfaction. She trembled, legs no longer dependable sup-ports beneath her, and yet in all her life she had never been more shockingly aware of her own body. Her braless breasts were swelling beneath the denim shirt she wore, the tender nipples suddenly tightening to thrust with aching sensitivity against the rough grain of the fabric.

There was a sudden enormous jarring thud on the windowpane behind her. Startled, Maxie almost jumped a foot in the air, and even Angelos flinched.

'Relax...a football hit the window,' he groaned in ap-parent disbelief as he raised his dark, imperious head. 'It is now being retrieved by two grubby little boys.'

But Maxie wasn't listening. She had been plunged into sudden appalled confusion by the discovery that Angelos Petronides had both arms loosely linked round her and had come within treacherous inches of kissing her. Even worse, she realised, every fibre of her yearning body had been longing desperately for that kiss.

Jerking back abruptly from the proximity of his lean,

muscular frame, Maxie pressed shaking hands against her hot, flushed cheeks. 'Get out of here and don't ever come back!'

Angelos grated something guttural in Greek, stood his ground and dealt her a hard, challenging look. 'What's the matter with you?'

And what remained of Maxie's self-respect drained away as she recognised his genuine bewilderment. Dear heaven, she had encouraged him. She had been straining up to him, mindlessly eager for his lovemaking, paralysed to the spot with excitement and longing, and he knew it too. And did his body feel as hers did now? Deprived, aching... As she registered such unfamiliar, intimate thoughts, Maxie realised just how out of control she was.

'I don't have to explain myself to you,' she gabbled in near panic as she rushed past him out into the hall to pull open the front door. 'I want you to leave and I don't want you to come back. In fact I'll put the dog on you if you ever come here again!'

In a demonstration of disturbing volatility, Angelos vented a sudden appreciative laugh, the sound rich and deep and earthy. His quality of dark implacability vanished under the onslaught of that amusement. Maxie stared. The sheer charisma of that wolfish grin took her by surprise.

'The dog's more likely to lick me to death...and you?' An ebullient ebony brow elevated as he watched the hot colour climb in her perplexed face.

'Leave!' The word erupted from Maxie, so desperate was she to silence him.

'And *you*?' Angelos repeated with steady emphasis. 'For some strange reason, what just happened between us, which on my level was nothing at all, unnerved you, scared you...embarrassed you...'

As he listed his impressions Maxie watched him with a sick, sinking sensation in her stomach, for never before had she been so easily read, and never before had a man made her feel like a specimen on a slide under a microscope.

'Now why should honest hunger provoke shame?' Angelos asked softly. 'Why not pleasure?'

'Pleasure?'

'I do not presume to know your every thought...as yet,' Angelos qualified with precision. His brilliant eyes intent, he strolled indolently back into the fresh air. 'But surely when ambition and desire unite, you should be pleased?'

He left her with that offensive suggestion, striding down the path and out to the pavement where a uniformed chauffeur waited beside a long, dark limousine. The two wide-eyed and decidedly grubby little boys, one of whom was clutching the football, were trying without success to talk to the po-faced chauffeur. She watched as Angelos paused to exchange a laughing word with them, bending to their level with disconcerting ease. Disturbed by her own fascination, she slammed shut the door on her view.

He would be back; she knew that. She couldn't explain how but she knew it as surely as she knew that dawn came around every morning. Feeling curiously like someone suffering from concussion, she wandered aimlessly back down into the kitchen and was surprised to find Liz sitting there, her kindly face anxious.

'Bounce started whining behind the studio door. He must've heard you shouting. I came back into the house but naturally I didn't intrude when I realised it was just an argument,' Liz confided ruefully. 'Unfortunately, before I retreated again, I heard rather more than I felt comfortable hearing. You're a wretched dog, Bounce...your grovelling greeting to Angelos Petronides affected my judgement!'

'So you realised who my visitor was—?'

'Not initially, but my goodness I should've done!' Liz exclaimed feelingly. 'You've talked about Angelos Petronides *so* often—'

'Have I?' Maxie breathed with shaken unease, her cheeks burning.

Liz smiled. 'All the time you were criticising him and

complaining about his behaviour, I could sense how attracted you were to him...'

A hoarse laugh erupted from Maxie's dry throat. 'I wish you'd warned me. It hit me smack in the face when I wasn't prepared for it. Stupid, wretched chemistry, and I never even realised... I feel such an idiot now!' Eyes prickling with tears of reaction, she studied the table, struggling to reinstate her usual control. 'And I've got the most banging headache s-starting up...'

'Of course you have,' Liz murmured soothingly. 'I've never heard you yelling at the top of your voice before.'

'But then I have never hated anyone so much in my life as I hate Angelos Petronides,' Maxie confessed shakily. 'I wanted to kill him, Liz...I really wanted to kill him! Now I'm in debt to *him* instead of Leland—'

'I did hear him say that you didn't have to worry about that.'

Maxie's eyes flashed. 'If it takes me until I'm ninety, I'll pay him back every penny!'

'He may have hurt your pride, Maxie...but he was most emphatic about not wanting repayment. He sounded sincere to me, and surely you have to give him some credit for his generosity whether you choose to regard it as a debt or otherwise?' Liz reasoned with an air of frowning confusion. 'The man has to be *seriously* interested in you to make such a big gesture on your behalf—'

'Liz—' Maxie broke in with a pained half-smile.

'Do you think he might turn out to be the marrying kind?' the older woman continued with a sudden teasing smile.

That outrageous question made Maxie's jaw drop. 'Liz, for heaven's sake...are you nuts?' she gasped. 'What put that in your mind?'

'Your godmother's will—'

'Oh, that...forget that, Liz. That's yesterday's news. Believe me when I say that Angelos Petronides was not thinking along the lines of anything as...well, anything as lasting as marriage.' Mindful of her audience, Maxie chose her words carefully and suppressed a sigh over the older woman's romantic imagination. 'He is not romantically interested in me. He is not that sort of man. He's hard, he's icy cold—'

'He didn't sound cold on my doorstep...he sounded downright *keen*! You'd be surprised how much I can pick up from the nuances in a voice.'

Liz was rather innocent in some ways. Maxie really didn't want to get down to basics and spell out just how a big, powerful tycoon like Angelos Petronides regarded her. As a social inferior, a beautiful body, a target object to acquire for his sexual enjoyment, a *live* toy. Maxie shrank with revulsion and hated him all over again. 'Liz...he would be offended by the very suggestion that he would even consider a normal relationship with a woman who's been another man's mistress—'

'But you haven't *been* another man's mistress!'

Maxie ignored that point. After the horrendous publicity she had enjoyed, nobody would ever believe that now. 'To be blunt, Liz...all Angelos wants is to get me into bed!'

'Oh...' Liz breathed, and blushed until all her freckles merged. 'Oh, dear, no...you don't want to get mixed up with a man like that.'

Maxie lay in bed that night, listening to the distant sound of the traffic. She couldn't forgive herself for being attracted to a male like Angelos Petronides. It was impossible that she could *like* anything about him. 'A woman of your nature,' he had said. His one little slip. Wanton, available, already accustomed to trading her body in return for a luxurious lifestyle. That was what he had meant. Her heart ached and she felt as if she was bleeding inside. How had she ever sunk to the level where she had a reputation like that?

When Maxie had first been chosen as the image to launch a new range of haircare products, she had been a complete unknown and only eighteen years old. Although she had never had the slightest desire to be a model, she had let her father persuade her to give it a try and had swiftly found herself earning what had then seemed like enormous amounts of money.

However, once the novelty had worn off, she had loathed the backbiting pressure and superficiality of the modelling circuit. She had saved like mad and had planned to find another way to make a living.

But all the time, in the background of her life, her father had continued to gamble. Relying on her income as a safety net, he had, without her knowledge, begun playing for higher and higher stakes. To be fair, Leland's casino manager had cut off Russ Kendall's credit line the minute he'd suspected the older man was in over his head. Maxie had met Leland Coulter for the first time the day she settled her father's outstanding tab at his casino.

'You won't change the man, Maxie,' he had told her then. 'If he was starving, he would risk his last fiver on a bet. He has to be the one who wants to change.'

After that humiliating episode her father had made her so many promises. He had sworn blind that he would never gamble again but inevitably he had broken his word. And, barred from the reputable casinos, he had gone dangerously down-market to play high-rolling poker games in smoky back rooms with the kind of tough men who would happily break his fingers if he didn't pay his dues on time. That was when Maxie's life had come completely unstuck...

Having got himself into serious debt, and learning to his dismay that his daughter had no savings left after his previous demands, Russ had been very badly beaten up. He had lost a kidney. In his hospital bed, he had sobbed with shame and terror in her arms. He had been warned that if he didn't come up with the money he owed, he would be crippled the next time.

Distraught, Maxie had gone to Leland Coulter for advice. And Leland had offered her an arrangement. He would pay off her father's gambling debts and allow her to repay him

at her leisure on condition that she moved in with him. He
had been very honest about what he wanted. Not sex, he
had insisted. No, what Leland had craved most had been
the ego-boosting pleasure of being seen to possess a beautiful young woman, who would preside over his dinner table, act as his hostess, entertain his friends and always be
available to accompany him wherever he went.

It hadn't seemed so much to ask. Nobody else had been
prepared to loan her that amount of money. And she had
been so agonisingly grateful that her father was safe from
further harm. She hadn't seen the trap she was walking into.
She hadn't even been aware that Leland was a married man
until the headlines had hit the tabloids and taken her reputation away overnight. She had borne the blame for the
breakup of his marriage.

'Jennifer and I split up because *she* had an affair,' Leland
had admitted grudgingly when Maxie had roundly objected
to the anomalous situation he had put her in. 'But this way,
with you by my side, I don't feel like a fool...all right?'

And she had felt sorry for him then, right through the
protracted and very public battle he and his wife had had
over alimony and property. Jennifer and Leland had fought
each other every inch of their slow path to the divorce
court, yet a week before the hearing, when Leland had had
a heart attack, the only woman he had been able to think
about when he was convinced that he was at his last gasp
had, most tellingly, been his estranged wife. 'Go away,
leave me alone... I need Jennifer here... I don't want her
seeing you with me now!' he had cried in pathetic masculine panic.

And that had hurt. In a crazy way she had grown rather
fond of Leland, even of his silly showing-off and quirky
little vanities. Not a bad man, just a selfish one, like all the
men she had ever known, and she hoped he was happy now
that he was back with his Jennifer. But he had used her not
only to soothe his wounded vanity but also, and less for-
givably, she recognised now, as a weapon with which to

punish his unfaithful wife. And Maxie could not forget that, or forgive herself for the blind naivety that had allowed it to happen in the first place. Never, ever again, she swore, would she be *used*...

Early the next morning, Maxie helped Liz pack. Her friend was heading off to stay with friends in Devon. The fact that her house wouldn't be left empty during her absence was a source of great relief to Liz. The previous year her home had been burgled and her studio vandalised while she was away.

As soon as she had seen the older woman off, Maxie spent an hour slapping on make-up like war-paint and dressing up in style. Angelos Petronides needed a lesson and Maxie was determined to give it to him.

Mid-morning, she pawned the one piece of valuable jewellery she owned. She had been eleven when she'd found the Victorian bracelet buried in a box of cheap costume beads which had belonged to her mother. She had cried, guessing why the bracelet had been so well concealed. Even in the three short years of her marriage, her poor mother had doubtless learnt the hard way that when her husband was short of money he would sell anything he could get his hands on. Afterwards, Russ would be terribly sorry and ashamed, but by then it would be too late and the treasured possession would be gone. So Maxie had kept the bracelet hidden too.

And now it hurt so much to surrender that bracelet. It felt like a betrayal of the mother she could barely remember. But she desperately needed the cash and she had nothing else to offer. Angelos Petronides *had* to be shown that he hadn't bought her or any rights over her by settling Leland's loan. The sacrifice of her mother's bracelet, temporarily or otherwise, simply hardened Maxie's angry, bitter resolve.

Half an hour later, she strolled out of the lift on to the top floor of the skyscraper that housed the London headquarters of the vast Petronides organisation. She spared the receptionist barely a glance. She knew how to get attention.

'I want to see Angelos,' she announced.

'Miss…Miss Kendall?' The brunette was already on her feet, eyes opened wide in recognition: in a bold scarlet dress that caressed every curve, her spectacular hair rippling in a sheet of gold to her waist, and heels that elevated her to well over six feet, Maxie was extremely noticeable.

'I know where his office is.' Maxie breezed on down the corridor, the brunette darting after her with an incoherent gasp of dismay.

She flung wide his office door when she got there. Infuriatingly, it was empty. She headed for the boardroom, indifferent to the squawking receptionist, whose frantic pursuit had attracted the attention of another two secretarial staff.

Bingo! Maxie strolled through the boardroom's double doors. An entire room full of men in business suits swivelled at her abrupt entry and then gaped. Maxie wasn't looking at them. Her entire attention was for Angelos Petronides, already rising from his chair at the head of the long polished table, his expression of outrage shimmering in an instant into shocking impassivity. But she took strength from the stunned quality that had briefly lit those fierce black eyes of his.

'I want to see you now,' Maxie told him, sapphire-blue eyes firing a challenge.

'You could wait in Mr Petronides's office, just through here, Miss Kendall.' The quiet female intervention came from the slim older woman who had already rushed to cast invitingly wide the door which connected with her employer's office.

'Sorry, I don't want to wait,' Maxie delivered.

A blazing look of dark, simmering fury betrayed Angelos. It was the reaction of a male who had never before been subjected to a public scene. Maxie smiled sweetly. He couldn't touch her because she had nothing to lose. No money, no current employment, nothing but her pride and her wits. He should've thought of that angle. And, no matter what it took, she intended to make Angelos pay for the state he had put her in the day before.

In one wrathful stride, Angelos reached her side and closed a forceful hand round her narrow wrist. Maxie let out a squeal as if he had hurt her. Startled, he dropped her wrist again. In receipt of a derisive, unimpressed glance that would've made a lesser woman cringe, Maxie noted without surprise that Angelos was a quick study.

'Thank you,' she said, and meant it, and she strolled through to his big, luxurious office like a little lamb because now she knew he was coming too.

'Unexpected visitors with unpredictable behaviour are so enervating...don't you think?' Maxie trilled as she fell still by the side of his impressive desk.

Angelos swore in Greek, studying her with seething black eyes full of intimidation. 'You crazy—' His wide mouth hardened as he bit back the rest of that verbal assault with the greatest of visible difficulty. 'What the hell are you playing at?' he growled like a grizzly bear instead.

'I'm not playing, I'm *paying*!' With a flourish, Maxie opened her fingers above his desk and let drop the crushed banknotes in her hand. 'Something on account towards the loan. I can't be bought like a tin of beans off a supermarket shelf!'

'How dare you interrupt a business meeting?' Angelos launched at her full throttle. 'How *dare* you make a scene like that in my boardroom?'

Maxie tensed. She had never heard a man that angry. She had never seen a male with so dark a complexion look that pale. Nor had she ever faced a pair of eyes that slashed like bloodthirsty razors into her.

'You asked for it,' she informed him grittily. 'You embarrassed me yesterday. You made me feel *this* big...' With her thumb and her forefinger she gave him a literal dem-

onstration. 'You made me feel powerless and this is pay-
back time. You picked on the wrong woman!'

'Is this really the Ice Queen I'm dealing with?' Angelos
responded very, very drily.

'You'd burn the ice off the North Pole!' Maxie sizzled
back at him, wondering why he had now gone so still, why
his naturally vibrant skin tone was recovering colour, indeed why he didn't appear to be in a rage any more.

'Do you suffer from a split personality?'

'Did you really think you *knew* me just because you were
in the same room with me a handful of times?' Maxie flung
her head back and was dumbstruck by the manner in which
his narrowed gaze instantly clung to her cascading mane of
hair, and then roved on down the rest of her with
unconcealed appreciation. It struck her that Angelos
Petronides was so convinced that he was an innately superior being and so oversexed that he couldn't take a
woman seriously for five minutes.

Brilliant black eyes swooped up to meet hers again. 'No
way did you ever behave like this around Leland—'

'My relationship with him is none of your business,'
Maxie asserted with spirit. 'But, believe me, nobody has
ever insulted me as much as you did yesterday.'

'I find that very hard to believe.'

Involuntarily, Maxie flinched.

Immensely tall and powerful in his superbly tailored
silver-grey suit, Angelos watched her, not an informative
glimmer of any emotion showing now on that lean, strong,
hard-boned face. 'Since when has it been an insult for a
man to admit that he wants a woman?' he demanded with
derision.

'You frightened the life out of me telling me you'd paid
off that loan...you put me under pressure, then you tried
to move in for the kill like the cold, calculating womaniser
you are!' Maxie bit out not quite levelly, and, spinning on
her heel, she started towards the door.

'All exits are locked. You're trapped for the moment,' Angelos delivered softly.

Maxie didn't believe him until she had tried and failed to open the door. Then she hissed furiously, 'Open this door!'

'Why should I?' Angelos enquired, choosing that exact same moment to lounge indolently back against the edge of his desk, so cool, calm and confident that Maxie wanted to rip him to pieces. 'Presumably you came here to entertain me...and, although I have no tolerance for tantrums, you *do* look magnificent in that dress, and naturally I would like to know why I'm receiving this melodramatic response to my proposition.'

In one flying motion, Maxie spun back. 'So you admit that that's what it was?'

'I want you. It's only a matter of time until I get what I want,' Angelos imparted very quietly in the deadly stillness.

Maxie shivered. 'When the soft soap doesn't work, weigh in with the threats—'

'That *wasn't* a threat. I don't threaten women,' Angelos growled with a feral flash of white teeth. 'No woman has ever come to my bed under threat!'

Nobody could feign that much outrage. He was an Alpha male and not one modestly given to underestimating his own attractions. But then, he had it *all*, she conceded bitterly. Incredible looks and sex appeal, more money than he could spend in a lifetime and a level of intelligence that scorched and challenged.

Maxie shot him a look of violent loathing. 'You think you're so special, don't you? You thought I'd be flattered, ready to snatch at whatever you felt like offering...but you're no different from any of the other men who have lusted after me,' she countered with harsh clarity. 'And I've had plenty of practice dealing with your sort. I've looked like this since I was fourteen—'

'I'm grateful you grew up before our paths crossed,' Angelos breathed with deflating amusement.

At that outrageous comment, something inside Maxie just cracked wide open, and she rounded on him like a tigress. 'I shouldn't have had to cope with harassment at that age. Do you think I don't *know* that I'm no more real to a guy like you than a blow-up sex doll?' she condemned with raw, stinging contempt. 'Well, I've got news for you, Mr Petronides...I am not available to be any man's live toy. You want a toy, you go to a store and buy yourself a railway set!'

'I thought you'd respect the upfront approach,' Angelos confided thoughtfully. 'But then I could never have guessed that behind the front you put on in public you suffer from such low self-esteem...'

Utterly thrown by that response, and with a horrendous suspicion that this confrontation was going badly wrong shrilling through her, Maxie suddenly felt foolish.

'Don't be ridiculous...of course I don't,' she argued with ragged stress. 'But, whatever mistakes I've made, I have no intention of repeating them. Now, I've told you how I feel, so open that blasted door and let me out of here!'

Angelos surveyed her with burning intensity, dense lashes low on penetrating black eyes. 'If only it were that easy...'

But this time when Maxie's perspiring fingers closed round the handle the door sprang open, and she didn't stalk like a prowling queen of the jungle on her exit, she simply fled, every nerve in her too hot body jangling with aftershock.

CHAPTER THREE

WHAT had possessed her, what on *earth* had possessed her? Maxie asked herself feverishly over and over again as she walked. The rain came heavily—long, lazy June days of sunshine finally giving way to an unseasonal torrent which drenched her to the skin within minutes. Since she was too warm, and her temples still pounded with frantic tension, she welcomed that cooling rain.

Something had gone wildly off the rails in that office. Angelos had prevented her quick exit. He had withstood everything she threw at him with provocative poise. In fact, just like yesterday, the more out of control she had got, the calmer and more focused he had become. And he zipped from black fury to outrageous cool at spectacular and quite unnerving speed.

Melodramatic, yes, Maxie acknowledged. She had been. Inexplicably, she had gone off the deep end and hurled recriminations that she had never intended to voice. And, like the shrewd operator he was, Angelos Petronides had trained those terrifyingly astute eyes on her while she recklessly exposed private, personal feelings of bitter pain and insecurity.

It was stress which had done this to her. Leland's heart attack, the sudden resulting upheaval in her own life, the dreadful publicity, her godmother's death. The pressure had got to her and blown her wide open in front of a male who zeroed in on any weakness like a predator. Low self-esteem…she did *not* suffer from low self-esteem!

A limousine drew up several yards ahead of her in the quiet side-street she was traversing. Alighting in one fluid movement, Angelos ran exasperated eyes over her sodden appearance and grated, 'Get in out of the rain, you foolish woman…don't you even know to take shelter when it's wet?'

Swallowing hard on that in-your-face onslaught, Maxie pushed shaking fingers through the wet strands of hair clinging to her brow and answered him with a blistering look of charged defiance. 'Go drop yourself down a drain!'

'Will you scream assault if I just throw you in the car?' Angelos demanded with raw impatience.

A kind of madness powered Maxie then, adrenaline racing through her. She squared up to him, scarlet dress plastered to her fantastic body, the stretchy hemline riding up on her long, fabulous legs. She dared him with her furious eyes and her attitude and watched his powerful hands clench into fists of self-restraint—because of course he was far too clever to make a risky move like that.

'Why are you following me?' she breathed.

'I'm not into railway sets…too slow, too quiet,' Angelos confessed.

'I'm not into egocentric dominating men who think they know everything better than me!' Maxie slung back at him, watching his luxuriant ebony hair begin to curl in the steady rain, glistening crystalline drops running down his hard cheekbones. And she thought crazily, He's getting wet for me, and she liked that idea.

'If this is my cue to say I might change…sorry, no can do. I am what I am,' Angelos Petronides spelt out.

Stupid not to take a lift when she could have one, Maxie decided on the spur of the moment, particularly when she was beginning to feel cold and uncomfortable in her wet clothing. Sidestepping him, enjoying the awareness that she was rather surprising him, she climbed into the limousine.

The big car purred away from the kerb.

'I decided to make you angry because I want you to leave me alone,' Maxie told him truthfully.

'Then why didn't you stay away from me? Why did you get into this car?' Angelos countered with lethal precision.

In answer, Maxie made an instinctive and instantaneous shift across the seat towards the passenger door. But, before she could try to jump back out of the car, a powerful hand whipped out to close over hers and hold her fast. The limousine quickened speed.

Black eyes clashed with hers. 'Are you suicidal?' Angelos bit out crushingly.

Maxie shakily pulled free of his grasp.

The heavy silence clawed at her nerves. Such a simple question, such a lethally simple, clever question, yet it had flummoxed her. If she had truly wanted to avoid him, why *had* she let something as trivial as wet clothes push her back into his company?

Angelos extended a lean brown hand again, with the aspect of an adult taking reluctant pity on a sulky child. 'Come here,' he urged.

Without looking at him again, Maxie curled into the far corner of the back seat instead. His larger-than-life image was already engraved inside her head. She didn't know what was happening to her, why she was reacting so violently to him. Her own increasing turmoil and the suspicion that she was adrift in dangerously unfamiliar territory frankly frightened her. Angelos Petronides was bad news in every way for a woman like her. Avoiding him like the plague was the only common sense response. And she should've been freezing him out, not screaming at him.

With a languorous sigh, Angelos shrugged fluidly out of his suit jacket. Without warning he caught her hand and pulled her to him. Taken by surprise, Maxie went crazy, struggling wildly to untangle herself from those powerful fingers. 'Let go! What are you trying to—?'

'Stop it!' Angelos thundered down at her, and he released her again in an exaggerated movement, spreading both arms wide as if to demonstrate that he carried no offensive weapon. 'I don't like hysterical women.'

'I'm not…I'm not like that.' Maxie quivered in shock and stark embarrassment as he draped his grey jacket round her slim, taut shoulders. The silk lining was still warm from his body heat. The faint scent of him clung to the garment and her nostrils flared. Clean, husky male, laced with the merest tang of some citrus-based lotion. She lowered her damp head and breathed that aroma in deep. The very physicality of that spontaneous act shook her.

'You're as high-strung as some of my racehorses,' Angelos contradicted. 'Every time I come close you leap about a foot in the air—'

'I didn't yesterday,' she muttered with sudden lancing bitterness.

'You didn't get the chance…I crept up on you.' With a tormentingly sexy sound of indolent amusement, Angelos reached out his hands and closed them over the sleeves of the jacket she now wore, tugging on them like fabric chains of captivity to bring her to him.

'No!' Maxie gasped, wide-eyed, her hands flying up, only to find that the only place she could plant her palms was against his broad, muscular chest.

'If you like, you can bail out after the first kiss—no questions asked, no strings attached,' Angelos promised thickly.

Even touching him through his shirt felt so incredibly intimate that guilty quivers ran through her tautening length. He was so hot. Her fingers spread and then shifted over the tactile silk barrier, learning of the rough whorls of hair below the fabric and enthralled. She was used to being around male models with shiny shaven chests. She shivered deliciously, appallingly tempted to rip open the shirt and explore.

Heavily lidded black eyes lambent with sensual indulgence intercepted hers. 'You look like a guilty child with her hand caught in the biscuit tin,' he confided with a lazy smile.

At the power of that smile, the breath tripped in Maxie's throat, her pupils dilating. His proximity mesmerised her. She could see tiny gold lights in his eyes, appreciate the incredible silky length and luxuriance of those black lashes and the faint blue shadow on his strong jawline. The potency of her own fascination filled her with alarm. 'You're all wrong for me,' she said in breathless panic, like a woman trying to run through a swamp and inexplicably finding herself standing still and sinking fast.

'Prove it,' Angelos invited in that velvet-soft drawl that fingered down her spine like a caress. A confident hand pushed into her drying hair and curved to the nape of her neck. 'Prove that anything that feels this good could possibly be wrong for either of us.'

He was so stunningly gorgeous, she couldn't think straight. Her heartbeat seemed to be racing in her tight throat. The insidious rise of her own excitement was like a drowning, overwhelming wave that drove all before it. He dropped his eyes to the pouting distended buds clearly delineated by the clinging bodice of her dress and her face burned red.

Slowly Angelos tilted her back, his arms banding round her spine to support her, and, bending his dark, arrogant head, he pressed the mouth she craved on hers to the thrusting sensitivity of an aching nipple instead. Her whole body jumped, throat arching, head falling back, teeth clenching on an incoherent whimper of shock.

Angelos lifted her up again, black eyes blazing with primal male satisfaction. 'It hurts to want this much. I don't think you were familiar with the feeling…but *now* you are.'

Trembling, Maxie stared at him, sapphire eyes dark with shaken arousal. Cold fear snaked through her. He was playing with her just as he might have played with a toy. Using his carnal expertise he was taunting her, winding her up, demonstrating his sexual mastery.

'Don't touch me!' Her hand whipped up and caught him across one hard cheekbone, and then she froze in dismay at what she had done.

With striking speed Angelos closed his fingers round that offending hand, and slowly he smiled again. 'Frustration *should* make you angry.'

Beneath her strained and bemused gaze, he bent his glossy dark head and pressed his lips hotly to the centre of her stinging palm. It was electrifying. It was as if every tiny bit of her body was suddenly programmed to overreact. And then, while she was still struggling to comprehend the incredible strength of his power over her, he caught her to him with indolent assurance and simply, finally, kissed her.

Only there was nothing simple about that long-awaited kiss. It blew Maxie away with excitement. It was like no kiss she had ever received. That hard, sensual mouth connected with hers and instantly she needed to be closer to him than his own skin. Pulses pounding at an insane rate, she clutched at him with frantic hands, reacting to the violent need climbing inside her, craving more with every passing second.

And then it was over. Angelos studied her with burnished eyes of appreciation, all virile male strength and supremacy as he absorbed the passion-glazed blankness of her hectically flushed and beautiful face.

'Come on,' he urged her thickly.

She hadn't even realised the limousine had stopped. Now he was closing his jacket round her again with immense care, practically lifting her back out into the rain and the sharp fresh air which she drank in great thirsty gulps. She felt wildly disorientated. For timeless minutes the world beyond the limousine just hadn't existed for her. In confusion, she curved herself into the support of the powerful arm welded to her narrow back and bowed her head.

Without warning, Angelos tensed and vented a crushing oath, suddenly thrusting her behind him. Maxie looked up just in time to see a photographer running away from them. Simultaneously two powerfully built men sprinted from the car behind the limo and grabbed him before he could make it across to the other side of the street.

Angelos untensed again, straightening big shoulders. 'My security men will expose his film. That photo of us will never see the light of day.'

In a daze, Maxie watched that promise carried out. As a demonstration of ruthlessness it took her breath away. She had often wished that she could avoid the intrusive cameras of the paparazzi, but she had never seen in action the kind of brute power which Angelos exercised to protect his privacy.

And it was *his* privacy that he had been concerned about, she sensed. Certainly not hers. Why was it that she suspected that Angelos would go to great lengths to avoid being captured in newsprint by her side? Why was it that she now had the strongest feeling that Angelos was determined not to be seen in public with her?

Shivering with reaction at that lowering suspicion, she emerged from her tangled thoughts to find herself standing in a stark stainless steel lift. 'Where are we?' she muttered then, with a frown of bewilderment.

The doors sped soundlessly back on a vast expanse of marble flooring.

'My apartment…where else?'

Maxie flinched in dismay, her brain cranking back into sudden activity. If that paparazzo had escaped, he would've had a highly embarrassing and profitable picture of her entering Angelos Petronides's apartment wrapped intimately in his jacket. No prizes for guessing what people would've assumed. She just could not believe how stupid she had been.

'I thought you were taking me back to Liz's,' she admitted rather unsteadily.

Angelos angled up a mocking brow. 'I never said I was...and, after our encounter in the car, I confess that I prefer to make love in my own bed.'

Maxie could feel her teeth starting to chatter, her legs shaking. Like a whore, that was how she would've looked in that photo, and that was exactly how he was treating her.

'Maxie...' Angelos purred, reading her retreat and switching channel to high-powered sensual persuasion as he strolled with animal grace towards her, strong, hard-boned face amused. 'You think I'm likely to respect you more if you suggest that we should wait another week, another month? I have no time for outdated attitudes like that—'

'Obviously not.' Agreement fell like dropped stones from Maxie's tremulously compressed lips.

'And I cannot credit that you should feel any differently. We will still be together six months from now,' Angelos forecast reflectively. 'Possibly even longer. I burn for you in a way I haven't burned for a woman in a very long time.'

'Try a cold shower.' Ice-cool as her own shrinking flesh, Maxie stood there, chin tilting as high as she could hold it even though she felt as if she was falling apart behind her façade. She shrugged back her shoulders so that his jacket slid off and fell in a rejected heap on the floor. 'I'm not some bimbo you can bed before you even date me—'

'The original idea was only to offer you lunch...' A dark rise of blood accentuated the tautening slant of his bold, hard cheekbones as he made that admission.

'But why waste time feeding me?' Maxie completed for him, her distaste unconcealed. 'In my time I have met some fast movers, but you have to qualify as supersonic. A kiss in the limo and that was consent to the whole menu?'

Angelos flung his arrogant dark head back, black eyes thudding like steel arrows into a target. 'The desire between us was honest and mutual and very strong. Do you expect me to apologise for a hunger you answered with a passion as powerful as my own?'

Maxie flinched. 'No...I don't think you make a habit of apologising.'

'I'm very straight...what you see is what you get. You put out conflicting signals and then back off. You have the problem,' Angelos informed her in cool condemnation. 'Don't put it on me. When I became an adult, I put childish games behind me.'

Although every strained muscle in her taut length ached, Maxie remained as outwardly poised as a queen surveying a less than satisfactory subject. But violent loathing powered her now. It took its strength from her shame that she had allowed him to touch her at all.

'I won't say it's been nice getting to know you over the past twenty-four hours, Angelos...it's been lousy,' Maxie stated, and turned in the direction of the lift.

'Goddamn you...don't you dare walk away from me!' Angelos slashed across the distance that separated them. 'Who are you, Maxie Kendall, to speak to *me* like that?'

'No more...I don't want to hear it,' Maxie muttered shakily.

'This time you will listen to me,' Angelos raked at her in wrathful forewarning. In one powerful stride he imposed his intimidating size between her and the lift. His lean, strong face hard as steel, bold black eyes hurled a ferocious challenge. 'Do you think I don't know you moved in with Leland between one day and the next? You hardly knew him. You came out of nowhere into his life. Do you think I didn't notice that you weren't remotely attracted to him?'

Quite unprepared for that angle of attack, Maxie stammered, 'I...I—'

'In fact, Leland bored you to death and you couldn't hide it. You could hardly bear him to touch you but you stuck it for three years all the same. Does that strike you as the behaviour of a sensitive woman with principles? You sold yourself for a wardrobe of designer clothes—'

'No, I didn't!' Maxie gasped strickenly.

'At no stage did you wake up and say to yourself, "I could do better than this. I'm worth more than this. This isn't the way I should be living!"' Angelos roared at her in a rage of shockingly raw derision. 'So don't tell me I got the wrong impression. I trust the evidence of my own eyes and senses. You felt nothing for him. But you put yourself on the market and he was still able to buy!'

Nausea stirring in her stomach, Maxie was retreating deeper into the penthouse apartment, her hands coming up in a fluttering movement in front of her as if she could somehow ward him off. 'No…no,' she mumbled sickly.

'And I was the bloody fool who, even knowing all that, *still* wanted you!' Angelos slung, spreading his arms in an extravagant gesture of outrage at her, at himself. 'I didn't want to buy you…or maybe I wanted the cosy pretence that it didn't have to be like that between us…that because you lusted after me too I could gloss over the knowledge that my immense wealth might have anything to do with your presence in my life!'

Maxie was like a statue, terrified to risk a step in case she cracked and broke into shattered pieces. He had forced her into cruel confrontation with the image he had of her. Like an explosion of glass, countless shards pierced her cringing flesh as every painful word drew blood.

'I'll never forgive you for this,' she whispered, more to herself than to him. 'But Leland was never my lover. We had an agreement. It was a charade we played—'

Angelos spat something guttural in Greek. 'Don't talk to me like I'm stupid!'

Maxie looked through him then, and despised herself for even attempting self-defence. It suggested a weakness inside her, a need for this arrogant Greek's good opinion that her savaged pride could not allow. 'You stay away from me from now on—'

'You made your choices in life long before you met me. What is it that you want now?' Angelos demanded contemptuously.

A semi-hysterical laugh erupted from Maxie and she choked it off, twisting her head away defensively before he could see the burning tears in her eyes. 'Just the usual things.' Then she whipped her golden head back, shimmering eyes as unwittingly bright as stars. 'And some day, when all this is behind me, I'll have them. I wouldn't have you as a gift, Angelos. I wouldn't make love with you unless you tied me to the bed and held me down and forced me...is that clear enough? What you want you will *never* have!'

Angelos stared at her as if he couldn't take his eyes off her and hated her for it.

Maxie stared back with a stab of malicious satisfaction new to her experience. 'Bad news, eh? I'll be the one who got away,' she breathed tautly, frighteningly aware of the thunderous charge of violence in the atmosphere but unable to silence her own tongue and her helpless need to taunt him. 'But then why should that bother you? It's not like you have a shred of *real* emotion in you—'

'What do you want from me?' Angelos ripped back at her with suppressed savagery. 'I will not and could not love a woman like you!'

'Oh, that honesty...hits me right where it hurts,' Maxie trilled, a knife-like pain scything through her. She was shaking like a leaf without even being aware of it. 'But for all that you still want me, don't you? Do you know something, Angelos? I *like* knowing that.'

A muscle jerked at the corner of his wide, sensual mouth, his strong jawline clenching. Those stunning black eyes burned with rage and seething pride.

'Thanks, you've just done wonders for my low self-esteem,' Maxie informed him with a jagged catch in her voice.

'What a bitch you can be...I never saw that in you before.' His accent was so thick she could have sliced it up, but that contemptuous intonation would still have flamed over her like acid, hurting wherever it touched. 'So, quote me a price for one night in your bed. What do you think you would be worth?'

The derisive suggestion coiled like a whip around her and scarred her worse than a beating. Her backbone went rigid. Hatred fired her embittered gaze. 'You couldn't even make the bidding,' Maxie asserted, looking him up and down as if he had crawled out from under a stone. 'I'd want a whole lot more than a wardrobe of designer clothes. You see, I learn from my mistakes, Angelos. The next man I live with will be my husband...'

Shock turned Angelos satisfying pale. 'If you think for one *insane* second that I—'

'Of course you wouldn't,' Maxie slotted in, each word clipped and tight with self-control. 'But you must see now why I'm not available for lunch, in bed or out of it. A woman can't be too careful. Being associated with a randy Greek billionaire could be very harmful to my new image.'

'I will work this entire dialogue out of your wretched hide every day you are with me!' Angelos snarled at her with primal force, all cool abandoned.

'You are just so slow on the uptake. I am not ever going to be *with* you, Angelos,' Maxie pointed out, and with that last word she strolled past him, holding herself taut and proud to the last, and walked into the lift.

Outside in the street again, she discovered that she was trembling so violently it was an effort to put one leg in front of the other. For once disregarding her straitened circumstances, she chose to hail a cab. Her mind was working like a runaway express train, disconnected images bombarding her...

How *could* two people who scarcely knew each other spend so long tearing each other apart? How could she have been that bitchy? How could she have actually enjoyed striking back at him and watching him react with impotent black fury? And yet now she felt sick at the memory, and astonishingly empty, like someone who had learned to thrive on electric tension and pain...and who now could not see a future worth living without them.

Angelos Petronides had devastated her but he wouldn't bother her again now, she told herself in an effort at consolation. Even the toughest male wouldn't put himself in line for more of the same. And Angelos least of all. He had expected her to fall into his bed with the eagerness of an avaricious bimbo, scarcely able to believe her good fortune. Instead she had hit that boundless ego of his, watched him shudder in sheer shock from the experience...and yet inside herself she felt the most awful bewildering sense of loss.

Reluctant to dwell on reactions that struck her as peculiar, Maxie chose instead to look back on their brief acquaintance with self-loathing. She squirmed over her own foolishness. Like an adolescent fighting a first powerful crush, she had overreacted every step of the way.

She had fancied him like mad but, blind and naive as a headstrong teenager, she hadn't even admitted that to herself until it was too late to save face. 'I have not been unaware of your interest in me.' She shuddered with shame. Had she surrendered to that physical attraction, it would've been a one-way ticket to disaster. She knew she couldn't afford to make any more wrong choices. She hadn't needed *him* to tell her that. Dear heaven, as if becoming his mistress would've been any kind of improvement on the humiliating charade Leland had forced her to live for so long!

Angelos hadn't believed her about Leland, of course he hadn't—hadn't even paused to catch his breath and listen. And in pushing the issue she would've made an ass of herself, for nothing short of medical proof of her virginity, if there was such a thing, would've convinced him otherwise. In any case the level of her experience wouldn't count with a male like Angelos Petronides. He viewed her the same way people viewed a takeaway snack. As something quick and cheap to devour, not savour. Her stomach lurched sickly. Even had she been tempted, which she hadn't been, had he thought for one moment that she would've believed she was likely to hold his interest as long as six months?

'A man will tell a girl who looks like you *anything* to get her into the bedroom,' her father had once warned her grimly. 'The one who is prepared to wait, the one who is more interested in how you feel, is the one who *cares.*'

That blunt advice had embarrassed her at a time when she was already struggling to cope with the downside of the spectacular looks she had been born with. Girlfriends threatened by the male attention she attracted had dumped her. Grown men had leered at her and tried to touch her and date her. Even teenage boys who, alone with her, had been totally intimidated by her, had told crude lies about her sexual availability behind her back. Eight years on, Maxie was still waiting without much hope to meet a man who wasn't determined to put the cart before the proverbial horse.

An hour after she got back to Liz's house, the phone rang. It was Catriona Ferguson, who ran the Star modelling agency which had first signed Maxie up at eighteen.

'I've got no good news for you, Maxie,' she shared in her usual brisk manner. 'The PR people over at LFT Haircare have decided against using you for another series of ads.'

'We were expecting that,' Maxie reminded the older woman with a rueful sigh of acceptance.

'I'm afraid there's nothing else in the pipeline for you. Hardly surprising, really,' Catriona told her. 'You're too strongly associated with one brand name. I did warn you about that risk and, to be blunt, your recent coverage in the tabloids has done you no favours.'

It had been a month since Maxie had moved out of Leland's townhouse. She hadn't worked since then and now it looked as if she was going to have to find some other means of keeping herself. Her bank account was almost empty. She couldn't afford to sit waiting for work that might never come, nor could she blame Catriona for her lack of sympathy. Time and time again the older woman had urged Maxie to branch out into fashion modelling, but Leland's frantic social life and the demands he had made on her time had made that impossible.

Hours later, Maxie hunched over both bars of the electric fire in Liz's lounge as she tried to keep warm while she brooded. Angelos was gone. That was good, she told herself, that was one major problem solved. She scratched an itchy place on her arm and then gazed down in surprise at the little rash of spots there.

What had she eaten that had disagreed with her? she wondered, but she couldn't recall eating anything more than half a sandwich since breakfast time. She just couldn't work up an appetite. She fell asleep on the settee and at some timeless stage of the night wakened to feel her way down to the guest-room and undress on the spot before sinking wearily into bed.

When she woke up late the next morning, she wasn't feeling too good. As she cleaned her teeth she caught a glimpse of her face in the tiny mirror Liz had on the wall for visitors and she froze. There was another little rash of spots on her forehead. It looked remarkably like... chickenpox. And she itched, didn't she? But only children got that, didn't they? And then she remembered one of Liz's neighbours calling in a couple of weeks back with a child in tow who had borne similiar spots.

'She's not infectious any more,' the woman had said carelessly.

Lower lip wobbling, Maxie surveyed the possible proof of that misapprehension. A dry cough racked her chest, leaving her gasping for breath. Whatever she had, she was feeling foul. Getting herself a glass of water, she went back to bed. The phone went. She had to get out of bed again to answer it.

'What?' she demanded hoarsely after another bout of coughing in the cold hall.

'Angelos here, what's wrong with you?'

'I have…I have a cold,' she lied. 'What do you want?'

'I want to see you—'

'No way!' Maxie plonked down the phone at speed.

The phone rang again. She disconnected it from its wall-point. A couple of hours later the doorbell went. Maxie ignored it. Getting out of bed yet again felt like too much trouble.

She dozed for the rest of the day, finally waking up shivering with cold and conscious of an odd noise in the dim room. Slowly it dawned on her that the rasping wheeze was the sound of her own lungs straining to function. Her brain felt befogged, but she thought that possibly she might need a doctor. So she lay thinking about that while the doorbell rang and rang and finally fell silent.

Fear got a healthy grip on her when she stumbled dizzily out of bed and her legs just folded beneath her. She hit the polished wooden floor with a crash. Tears welled up in her sore eyes. The room was too dark for her to get her bearings. She started to crawl, trying to recall where the phone was. She heard a distant smash. It sounded like glass breaking, and then voices. Had she left the television on? Trying to summon up more strength, she rested her perspiring brow down on the boards beneath her.

And then the floor lit up…or so it seemed.

CHAPTER FOUR

A DISTURBINGLY familiar male voice bit out something raw in a foreign language and a pair of male feet appeared in Maxie's limited view. Strong hands turned her over and began to lift her.

'You're all...*spotty*...' Angelos glowered down at her with unblinking black eyes, full of disbelief.

'Go away...' she mumbled.

'It just looks a little...strange,' Angelos commented tautly, and after a lengthy pause, while Maxie squeezed shut her eyes against the painful intrusion of that overhead light *and* him, he added almost accusingly, 'I thought only children got chickenpox.'

'Leave me alone...' Maxie succumbed weakly to another coughing fit.

Instead, he lifted her back onto the bed and rolled the bulky duvet unceremoniously round her prone body.

'What are you doing?' she gasped, struggling to concentrate, finding it impossible.

'I was on my way down to my country house for the weekend. Now it looks like I'll be staying in town and you'll be coming home with me,' Angelos delivered, with no visible enthusiasm on his strong, hard face as he bent down to sweep her up into his powerful arms.

Maxie couldn't think straight, but the concept of having nothing whatsoever to do with Angelos Petronides was now so deeply engrained, his appearance had set all her alarm bells shrieking. 'No...I have to stay here to look after the house—'

'I wish you could...but you can't.'

'I promised Liz…she's away and she might be burgled again…put me down.'

'I can't leave you alone here like this.' Angelo stared down at her moodily, as if he was wishing she would make his day with a sudden miraculous recovery but secretly knew he didn't have much hope.

Maxie struggled to conceal her spotty face against his shoulder, mortified and weak, and too ill to fight but not too ill to hate. 'I don't want to go anywhere with you.' Gulping, she sniffed.

'I don't see any caring queue outside that door ready to take my place…and what have you got to snivel about?' Angelos demanded with stark impatience as he strode down the hall. Then he stopped dead, meshing long fingers into her hair to tug her face round and gaze accusingly down into her bemused eyes. 'I smashed my way in only because I was aware that you were ill. Decency demanded that I check that you were all right.'

'I do not snivel,' Maxie told him chokily.

'But the only reason I came here tonight was to return your "something on account" and to assure you that it would be a cold day in hell before I ever darkened your door again—'

'So what's keeping you?'

But Angelos was still talking like a male with an ever-mounting sense of injustice. 'And there you are, lying on the floor in a pathetic shivering heap with more spots than a Dalmatian! What's fair about that? But I'm not snivelling, am I?'

Maxie opened one eye and saw one of his security men watching in apparent fascination. 'I do not snivel…' she protested afresh.

Angelos strode out into the night air. He ducked down into the waiting limousine and propped Maxie up in the farthest corner of the seat like a giant papoose that had absolutely nothing to do with him.

Only then did Maxie register that the limousine was already occupied by a gorgeous redhead, wearing diamonds and a spectacular green satin evening dress which would've been at home on the set of a movie about the Deep South of nineteenth-century America. The other woman gazed back at Maxie, equally nonplussed.

'Have you had chickenpox, Natalie?' Angelos enquired almost chattily.

Natalie Cibaud. She was an actress, a well-known French actress, who had recently won rave reviews for her role in a Hollywood movie. It had not taken Angelos long to find other more entertaining company, Maxie reflected dully while a heated conversation in fast and furious French took place. Maxie didn't speak French, but the other woman sounded choked with temper while Angelos merely got colder and colder. Maxie curled up in an awkward heap, conscious she was the subject under dispute and wishing in despair that she could perform a vanishing act.

'Take me home!' she cried once, without lifting her sore head.

'Stay out of this…what's it got to do with you?' Angelos shot back at her with positive savagery. 'No woman owns me…no woman ever has and no woman ever will!'

But Angelos was fighting a losing battle. Natalie appeared to have other ideas. Denied an appropriately humble response, her voice developed a sulky, shrill edge. Angelos became freezingly unresponsive. Strained silence finally fell. A little while later, the limousine came to a halt. The passenger door opened. Natalie swept out with her rustling skirts, saying something acid in her own language. The door slammed again.

'I suppose you thoroughly enjoyed all that,' Angelos breathed in a tone of icy restraint as the limousine moved off again.

Opening her aching eyes a crack, Maxie skimmed a dulled glance at the space Natalie had occupied and recently vacated. She closed her eyes again. 'I don't understand French…'

Angelos grated something raw half under his breath and got on the phone. He had been ditched twice in as many days. And, wretched as she was, Maxie was tickled pink by that idea. Angelos, who got chased up hill and down dale by ninety-nine out of a hundred foolish women, had in the space of forty-eight hours met two members of the outstanding and more intelligent one per cent minority. And it was good for him—really, really good for him, she decided. Then she dozed, only to groggily resurface every time she coughed. Within a very short time after that, however, she didn't know where she was any more and felt too ill to care.

'Feeling a bit better, Miss Kendall?'

Maxie peered up at the thin female face above hers. The face was familiar, and yet unfamiliar too. The woman wore a neat white overall and she was taking Maxie's pulse. Seemingly she was a nurse.

'What happened to me?' Maxie mumbled, only vaguely recalling snatches of endless tossing and turning, the pain in her chest, the difficulty in breathing.

'You developed pneumonia. It's a rare but potentially serious complication,' the blonde nurse explained. 'You've been out of it for almost five days—'

'Five…days?' Maxie's shaken scrutiny wandered over the incredibly spacious bedroom, with its stark contemporary furniture and coldly elegant decor. She was in Angelos's apartment. She knew it in her bones. Nowhere was there a single piece of clutter or feminine warmth and homeliness. His idea of housing heaven, she reflected absently, would probably be the wide open spaces of an under-furnished aircraft hangar.

'You're very lucky Mr Petronides found you in time,' her companion continued earnestly, dragging Maxie back

from her abstracted thoughts. 'By recognising the serious-
ness of your condition and ensuring that you got immediate
medical attention, Mr Petronides probably saved your
life—'

'No...I don't want to owe him *anything*...never mind
my life!' Maxie gasped in unconcealed horror.

The slim blonde studied her in disbelief. 'You've been
treated by one of the top consultants in the UK...Mr
Petronides has provided you with the very best of round-
the-clock private nursing care, and you say—?'

'While Miss Kendall is ill, she can say whatever she
likes,' Angelos's dark drawl slotted in grimly from the far
side of the room. 'You can take a break, Nurse. I'll stay
with your patient.'

The woman had jerked in dismay at Angelos's silent entrance and intervention. Face pink, she moved away from
the bed. 'Yes, Mr Petronides.'

In a sudden burst of energy, Maxie yanked the sheet up
over her head.

'And the patient is remarkably lively all of a sudden,'
Angelos remarked as soon as the door closed on the nurse's
exit. 'And ungrateful as hell. Now, why am I not surprised?'

'Go away,' Maxie mumbled, suddenly intensely conscious of lank sweaty hair and spots which had probably
multiplied.

'I'm in my own apartment,' Angelos told her drily. 'And
I am not going away. Do you seriously think that I haven't
been looking in on you to see how you were progressing
over the past few days?'

'I don't care...I'm properly conscious now. If I was so
ill, why didn't you just take me to hospital?' Maxie demanded from beneath the sheet.

'The top consultant is a personal friend. Since you responded well to antibiotics, he saw no good reason to
move you.'

'Nobody consulted me,' Maxie complained, and shifted to scratch an itchy place on her hip.

Without warning, the sheet was wrenched back.

'No scratching,' Angelos gritted down at her with raking impatience. 'You'll have scars all over you if you do that. If I catch you at that again, I might well be tempted to tie your hands to the bed!'

Aghast at both the unveiling and the mortifying tone of that insultingly familiar threat, Maxie gazed up at him with outraged blue eyes bright as jewels. 'You pig,' she breathed shakily, registering that he was getting a kick out of her embarrassment. 'You had no right to bring me here—'

'You're in no fit state to tell me what to do,' Angelos reminded her with brutal candour. 'And even I draw the line at arguing with an invalid. If it's of any comfort to your wounded vanity, I've discovered that once I got used to the effect the spotty look could be surprisingly appealing.'

'Shut up!' Maxie slung at him, and fell back against the pillows, completely winded by the effort it had taken to answer back.

While she struggled to even out her breathing, she studied him with bitter blue eyes. Angelos looked soul-destroyingly spectacular. He wore a beige designer suit with a tie the shade of rich caramel and a toning silk shirt. The lighter colours threw his exotic darkness into prominence. He exuded sophistication and exquisite cool, and at a moment when Maxie felt more grotty than she had ever felt in her life, she loathed him for it! Rolling over, she presented him with her back.

Maddeningly, Angelos strolled round the bed to treat her to an amused appraisal. 'I'm flying over to Athens for the next ten days. I suspect you'll recover far more happily in my absence.'

'I won't be here when you get back…oh, no, Liz's house

has been left empty!' Maxie moaned in sudden guilty dismay.

'I had a professional housesitter brought in.'

Maxie couldn't even feel grateful. Her heart sank even further. He had settled Leland's loan. He had paid for expensive private medical care within his own home. And now he had shelled out for a housesitter as well. If it took her the rest of her life, she would still be paying off what she now had to owe him in total!

'Thanks,' she muttered ungraciously, for her friend's sake.

'Don't mention it,' Angelos said with considerable irony. 'And you *will* be here when I return. If you're not, I'll come looking for you in a very bad mood—'

'Don't talk like you own me!' she warned him in feverish, frantic denial. 'You were with that actress only a few days ago...you were never going to darken my door again—'

'You darkened mine. Oh...yes, before I forget...' Angelos withdrew something small and gold from his pocket and tossed it carelessly on the bed beside her.

Stunned, Maxie focused on the bracelet which she had pawned.

'"*Ice Queen in pawnshop penury*" ran the headline in the gossip column,' Angelos recounted with a sardonic elevation of one ebony brow as he watched Maxie turn brick-red with chagrin. 'The proprietor must've tipped off the press. I found the ticket in your bag and had the bracelet retrieved.'

Wide-eyed and stricken, Maxie just gaped at him.

Angelos dealt her a scorching smile of reassurance. 'You won't have to endure intrusive publicity like that while you are with me. I will protect you. You will never have to enter a pawnshop again. Nor will you ever have to shake your tresses over a misty green Alpine meadow full of wildflowers...unless you want to do it for my benefit, of course.'

Maxie simply closed her eyes on him. She didn't have the energy to fight. He was like a tank in the heat and fury of battle. Nothing short of a direct hit by a very big gun would stop his remorseless progress.

'Silence feels good,' Angelos remarked with silken satisfaction.

'I hate you,' Maxie mumbled, with a good deal of very real feeling.

'You hate *wanting* me,' Angelos contradicted with measured emphasis. 'It's poetic justice and don't expect sympathy. When I had to think of you lying like a block of ice beneath Leland, I did not enjoy wanting you either!'

Maxie buried her burning face in the pillow with a hoarse little moan of self-pity. He left her nothing to hide behind. And any minute now she expected to be hauled out of concealment. Angelos preferred eye-to-eye contact at all times.

'Get some sleep and eat plenty,' Angelos instructed from somewhere alarmingly close at hand, making her stiffen in apprehension. 'You should be well on the road to recovery by the time I get back from Greece.'

Maxie's teeth bit into the pillow. Her blood boiled. For an instant she would have sacrificed the rest of her life for the ability to punch him in the mouth just once. She thought he had gone, and lifted her head. But Angelos, who never, ever, it seemed, did anything she expected, was still studying her from the door, stunning dark features grave. 'By the way, I also expect you to be extremely discreet about this relationship—'

'We don't have a relationship!' Maxie bawled at him. 'And I wouldn't admit to having been here in your apartment if the paparazzi put thumbscrews on me!'

Angelos absorbed that last promise with unhidden satisfaction. And then, with a casual inclination of his dark, arrogant head, he was gone, and she slumped, weak and shaken as a mouse who had been unexpectedly released from certain death by a cat.

Maxie finished packing her cases. While she had been ill, Angelos had had all her clothes brought over from Liz's. The discovery had infuriated her. A few necessities would have been sensible, but *everything* she possessed? Had he really thought she would be willing to stay on after she recovered?

For the first thirty-six hours after his departure she had fretted and fumed, struggling to push herself too far too fast in her eagerness to vacate his unwelcome hospitality.

The suave consultant had made a final visit to advise her to take things slowly, and the shift of nursing staff had departed, but Maxie had had to face that she was still in no fit state to look after herself. So she *had* been sensible. She had taken advantage of the opportunity to convalesce and recharge her batteries while she was waited on hand and foot by the Greek domestic staff…but now she was leaving before Angelos returned. In any case, Liz was coming home at lunchtime.

Two of Angelos's security men were hovering in the vast echoing entrance hall. Taut with anxiety, they watched her stagger towards them with her suitcases. Neither offered an ounce of assistance.

'Mr Petronides is not expecting——' the bigger, older one finally began stiffly.

'If you know what's good for you, you'll stay out of this!' Maxie thumped the lift button with a clenched fist of warning.

'Mr Petronides doesn't want you to leave, Miss Kendall. He's going to be annoyed.'

Maxie opened dark blue eyes very, very wide. *'So?'*

'We'll be forced to follow you, Miss Kendall——'

'Oh, I wouldn't do that, boys,' Maxie murmured gently. 'I would hate to call in the police because I was being harassed by stalkers. It would be sure to get into the papers too, and I doubt that your boss would enjoy *that* kind of publicity!'

In the act of stepping forward as the lift doors folded back, both men froze into frustrated stillness. Maxie dragged her luggage into the lift.

'A word of advice,' the older one breathed heavily. 'He makes a relentless enemy.'

Maxie tossed her head in a dismissive movement. Then the doors shut and she sagged. No wonder Angelos threw his weight around so continually. Everybody was terrified of him. Unlimited wealth and power had made him what he was. His ruthless reputation chilled, his lethal influence threatened. The world had taught him that he could have whatever he wanted. Only not her...never ever *her*, she swore vehemently. Her mind was her own. Her body was her own. She was inviolate. Angelos couldn't touch her, she reminded herself bracingly.

The housesitter vacated Liz's house after contacting her employer for instructions. Alone then, and tired out by the early start to the day, Maxie felt very low. Making herself a cup of coffee, she checked through the small pile of post in the lounge. One of the envelopes was addressed to her; it had been redirected.

The letter appeared to be from an estate agent. Initially mystified, Maxie struggled across the barrier of her dyslexia to make sense of the communication. The agent wrote that he had been unable to reach her father at his last known address but that she had been listed by Russ as a contact point. He required instructions concerning a rental property which was now vacant. Memories began to stir in Maxie's mind.

Her father's comfortably off parents had died when she was still a child. A black sheep within his own family even then, Russ had inherited only a tiny cottage on the outskirts of a Cambridgeshire village. He had been even less pleased to discover that the cottage came with an elderly sitting tenant, who had not the slightest intention of moving out to enable him to sell up.

Abandoning the letter without having got further than the third line, Maxie telephoned the agent. 'I can't tell you where my father is at present,' she admitted ruefully. 'I haven't heard from him in some time.'

'The old lady has moved in with relatives. If your father wants to attract another tenant, he'll have to spend a lot on repairs and modernisation. However,' the agent continued with greater enthusiasm, 'I believe the property would sell very well as a site for building development.'

And of course that would be what Russ would want, Maxie reflected. He would sell and a few months down the road the proceeds would be gone again, wasted on the racecourse or the dog track. Her troubled face stiffening with resolve, Maxie slowly breathed in and found herself asking if it would be in order for her to come and pick up the keys.

She came off the phone again, so shaken by the ideas mushrooming one after another inside her head that she could scarcely think straight. But she *did* need a home, and she had always loved the countryside. If she had the courage, she could make a complete fresh start. Why not? What did she have left in London? The dying remnants of a career which had done her infinitely more harm than good? She could find a job locally. Shop work, bar work; she wasn't fussy. As a teenager Maxie had done both, and she had no false pride.

By the time Liz came home, Maxie was bubbling with excitement. In some astonishment, Liz listened to the enthusiastic plans that the younger woman had already formulated.

'If the cottage is in a bad way, it could cost a fortune to put it right, Maxie,' she pointed out anxiously. 'I don't want to be a wet blanket, but by the sound of things—'

'Liz…I never did want to be a model and I'm not getting any work right now,' Maxie reminded her ruefully. 'This could be my chance to make a new life and, whatever it takes, I want to give it a try. I'll tell the agency where I am so that if anything does come up they can contact me, but I certainly can't afford to sit around here doing nothing. At least if I start earning again, I can start paying back Angelos.'

If Maxie could've avoided telling Liz about the house-sitter and her own illness, she would've done so. But Liz had a right to know that a stranger had been looking after her home. However, far from being troubled by that revelation, Liz was much more concerned to learn that Maxie had been ill. She was also mortifyingly keen to glean every detail of the role which Angelos Petronides had played.

'I swear that man is madly in love with you!' Liz shook her head in wonderment.

Maxie vented a distinctly unamused laugh, her eyes incredulous. 'Angelos wouldn't know love if it leapt up and bit him to the bone! But he will go to any lengths to get what he wants. I suspect he thinks that the more indebted he makes me, the easier he'll wear down my resistance—'

'Maxie…if he'd left you lying here alone in this house, you might be dead. Don't you even feel the slightest bit grateful?' Liz prompted uncomfortably. 'He could've just called an ambulance—'

'Thereby missing out on the chance to get me into his power when I was helpless?' Maxie breathed cynically. 'No way. I know how he operates. I *know* how he thinks.'

'Then you must have much more in common with him than you're prepared to admit,' Liz commented.

Maxie arrived at the cottage two days later. With dire mutters, the cabbie nursed his car up the potholed lane. In the sunshine, the cottage looked shabby, but it had a lovely setting. There was a stream ten feet from the front door and a thick belt of mature trees that provided shelter.

She had some money in her bank account again too. She had liquidated a good half of her wardrobe. Ruthlessly piling up all the expensive designer clothes which Leland had insisted on buying her, Maxie had sold them to a couple of those wonderful shops which recycle used quality garments.

Half an hour later, having explored her new home, Maxie's enthusiasm was undimmed. So what if the accommodation was basic and the entire place crying out for paint and a seriously good scrub? As for the repairs the agent had mentioned, Maxie was much inclined to think he had been exaggerating.

She was utterly charmed by the inglenook fireplace in the little front room and determined not to take fright at the minuscule scullery and the spooky bathroom with its ancient cracked china. Although the furnishings were worn and basic, there were a couple of quite passable Edwardian pieces. The new bed she had bought would be delivered later in the day.

She was about a mile from the nearest town. As soon as she had the bed made up, she would call in at the hotel she had noticed on the main street to see if there was any work going. In the middle of the tourist season, she would be very much surprised if there wasn't an opening somewhere...

Five days later, Maxie was three days into an evening job that was proving infinitely more stressful than she had anticipated. The pace of a waitress in a big, busy bar was frantic.

And why, oh, why hadn't she asked whether the hotel bar served meals *before* she accepted the job? She could carry drinks orders quite easily in her head, but she had been driven into trying to employ a frantic shorthand of numbers when it came to trying to cope at speed with the demands of a large menu and all the innumerable combinations possible. She just couldn't write fast enough.

Maxie saw Angelos the minute he walked into the bar. The double doors thrust back noisily. He made an entrance. People twisted their heads to glance and then paused to stare. Command and authority written in every taut line of his tall, powerful frame, Angelos stood out like a giant among pygmies.

Charcoal-grey suit, white silk shirt, smooth gold tie. He looked filthy rich, imposing and utterly out of place. And Maxie's heart started to go bang-bang-bang beneath her uniform. He had the most incredible traffic-stopping presence. Suddenly the crowded room with its low ceiling and atmospheric lighting felt suffocatingly hot and airless.

For a split second Angelos remained poised, black eyes raking across the bar to close in on Maxie. She had the mesmerised, panicked look of a rabbit caught in car headlights. His incredulous stare of savage impatience zapped her even at a distance of thirty feet.

Sucking in oxygen in a great gulp, Maxie struggled to finish writing down the order she was taking on her notepad. Gathering up the menus again, she headed for the kitchens at a fast trot. But it wasn't fast enough. Angelos somehow got in the way.

'Take a break,' he instructed in a blistering undertone.

'How the heck did you find out where I was?'

'Catriona Ferguson at the Star modelling agency was eager to please.' Angelos watched Maxie's eyes flare with angry comprehension. 'Most people are rather reluctant to say no to me.'

In an abrupt move, Maxie sidestepped him and hurried into the kitchen. When she re-emerged, Angelos was sitting at one of *her* tables. She ignored him, but never had she been more outrageously aware of being watched. Her body felt uncoordinated and clumsy. Her hands perspired and developed a shake. She spilt a drink and had to fetch another while the woman complained scathingly about the single tiny spot that had splashed her handbag.

Finally the young bar manager, Dennis, approached her. 'That big dark bloke at table six...haven't you noticed him?' he enquired apologetically, studying her beautiful face with the same poleaxed expression he had been wearing ever since he'd hired her. With an abstracted frown, he looked across at Angelos, who was tapping long brown fingers with rampant impatience on the tabletop. 'It's odd. There's something incredibly familiar about the bloke but I can't think where I've seen him before.'

Maxie forced herself over to table six. 'Yes?' she prompted tautly, and focused exclusively on that expensive gold tie while all the time inwardly picturing the derision in those penetrating black eyes.

'That uniform is so short you look like a bloody French maid in a bedroom farce!' Angelos informed her grittily. 'Every time you bend over, every guy in here is craning his neck to get a better view! And that practice appears to include the management.'

Maxie's face burned, outrage flashing in her blue eyes. The bar had a Victorian theme, and the uniform was a striped overall with a silly little frilly apron on top. It did look rather odd on a woman of her height and unusually long length of leg, but she had already let down the hemline as far as it would go. 'Do you or do you not want a drink?' she demanded thinly.

'I'd like the table cleared and cleaned first,' Angelos announced with a glance of speaking distaste at the cluttered surface. 'Then you can bring me a brandy and sit down.'

'Don't be ridiculous...I'm working.' Maxie piled up the dishes with a noisy clatter, and in accidentally slopping coffee over the table forced him to lunge back at speed from the spreading flood.

'You're working for me, and if I say you can sit down,

I expect you to do as you're told,' Angelos delivered in his deep, dark, domineering drawl.

Engaged in mopping up, Maxie stilled. 'I beg your pardon? You said…I was working for *you*?' she queried.

'This hotel belongs to my chain,' Angelos ground out. 'And I am anything but impressed by what I see here.'

Maxie turned cold with shock. Angelos *owned* this hotel? She backed away with the dishes. As she was hailed from the kitchen, she watched with a sinking stomach as Angelos signalled Dennis. When she reappeared with a loaded tray, Dennis was seated like a pale, perspiring graven image in front of Angelos.

She hurried to deliver the meals she had collected but there was a general outcry of loud and exasperated complaint.

'I didn't order this…' the first customer objected. 'I asked for salad, not French fries—'

'And I wanted garlic potatoes—'

'This steak is *rare*, not well-done—'

The whole order was hopelessly mixed up. A tall, dark shadow fell menacingly over the table. In one easy movement, Angelos lifted Maxie's pad from her pocket, presumably to check out the protests. 'What *is* this?' he demanded, frowning down at the pages as he flipped. 'Egyptian hieroglyphics…some secret code? Nobody could read this back!'

Maxie was paralysed to the spot; her face was bone-white. Her tummy lurched with nausea and her legs began to shake. 'I got confused, I'm sorry. I—'

Angelos angled a smooth smile at the irate diners and ignored her. 'Don't worry, it will be sorted out as quickly as possible. Your meals are on the house. Move, Maxie,' he added in a whiplike warning aside.

Dennis, she noticed sickly, was over at the bar using the internal phone. He looked like a man living a nightmare. And when she came out of the kitchen again, an older man, whom she recognised as the manager of the entire hotel, was with Angelos, and he had the desperate air of a man walking a tightrope above a terrifying drop. Suddenly Maxie felt like the albatross that had brought tragedy to an entire ship's crew. Angelos, it seemed, was taking out his black temper on his staff. Her own temper rose accordingly.

How the heck could she have guessed that he owned this hotel? She recalled the innumerable marble plaques in the huge foyer of the Petronides building in London. Those plaques had listed the components of Angelos's vast and diverse business empire. Petronides Steel, Petronides Property, and ditto Shipping, Haulage, Communications, Construction, Media Services, Investments, Insurance. No doubt she had forgotten a good half-dozen. PAI— Petronides Amalgamated Industries—had been somewhat easier to recall.

'Maxie...I mean, Miss Kendall,' Dennis said awkwardly, stealing an uneasy glance at her and making her wonder what Angelos had said or done to make him behave like that. But not for very long. 'Mr Petronides says you can take the rest of the night off.'

Maxie stiffened. 'Sorry, I'm working.'

Dennis looked aghast. 'But—'

'I was engaged to work tonight and I need the money.' Maxie tilted her chin in challenge.

She banged a brandy down in front of Angelos. 'You're nothing but a big, egocentric bully!' she slung at him with stinging scorn.

A lean hand closed round her elbow before she could stalk away again. Colour burnished her cheeks as Angelos forced her back to his side with the kind of male strength that could not be fought without making a scene. Black eyes as dark as the legendary underworld of Hades slashed threat into hers. 'If I gave you a spade, you would happily dig your own grave. Go and get your coat—'

'No...this is my job and I'm not walking out on it.'

'Let me assist you to make that decision. You're sacked...' Angelos slotted in with ruthless bite.

With her free hand, Maxie swept up the brandy and up-ended it over his lap. In an instant she was free. With an unbelieving growl of anger, Angelos vaulted upright.

'If you can't stand the heat, stay out of the kitchen!' Maxie flung fiercely, and stalked off, shoulders back, classic nose in the air.

CHAPTER FIVE

DENNIS was waiting for Maxie outside the staff-room when she emerged in her jeans and T-shirt. Pale and still bug eyed with shock, he gaped at her. 'You must be out of your mind to treat Angelos Petronides like that!'

'Envy me...I don't work for him any more.' Maxie flung her golden head high. 'May I have my pay now, please?'

'Y-your pay?' the young bar manager stammered.

'Is my reaction to being forcibly held to the spot by the owner of this hotel chain sufficient excuse to withhold it?' Maxie enquired very drily.

The silence thundered.

'I'll get your money...I don't really think I want to raise that angle with Mr Petronides right now,' Dennis confided weakly.

Ten minutes later Maxie walked out of the hotel, grimacing when she realised that it was *still* pouring with rain. It had been lashing down all day and she had got soaked walking into town in spite of her umbrella. Every passing car had splashed her. A long, low-slung sports car pulled into the kerb beside her and the window buzzed down.

'Get in,' Angelos told her in a positive snarl.

'Go take a hike! You can push around your staff but you can't push *me* around!'

'Push around? Surely you noticed how sloppily that bar was being run?' Angelos growled in disbelief. Thrusting open the car door, he climbed out to glower down at her in angry reproof. 'Insufficient and surly staff, customers kept waiting, the kitchens in chaos, the tables dirty and even the carpet in need of replacement! If the management don't

get their act together fast, I'll replace them. They're not
doing their jobs.'

Taken aback by his genuine vehemence, Maxie nonethe-
less suppressed the just awareness that she herself had been
less than impressed by what she had seen. He had changed
too, she noticed furiously. He must have had a change of
clothes with him, because now he was wearing a spectacular suit of palest grey that had the exquisite fit of a kid
glove on his lean powerful frame.

Powered by sizzling adrenaline alone, Maxie studied that
lean, strong face. 'I hate you for following me down
here—'

'You were waiting for me to show up...'

Her facial muscles froze. The minute Angelos said it, she
knew it was true. She had *known* he would track her down
and find her.

'I'm walking home. I'm not getting into your car,' she
informed him while she absently noted that, yet again, he
was getting wet for her. Black hair curling, bronzed cheekbones shimmering damply in the street lights.

'I have not got all night to waste, waiting for you to
walk home,' Angelos asserted wrathfully.

'So you know where I'm living,' Maxie gathered in
growing rage, and then she thought, What am I doing here
standing talking to him? 'Well, don't you dare come there
because I won't open the door!'

'You could be attacked walking down a dark country
road,' Angelos ground out, shooting her a flaming look of
antipathy. 'Is it worth the risk?'

Angling her umbrella to a martial angle, Maxie spun on
her heel and proceeded to walk. She hadn't gone ten yards
before her flowing hair and long easy stride attracted the
attention of a bunch of hard-faced youths lounging in a
shop doorway. Their shouted obscenities made her stiffen
and quicken her pace.

From behind her, she heard Angelos grate something savage.

A hand came down without warning on Maxie's tense shoulder and she uttered a startled yelp. As she attempted to yank herself free, everything happened very fast. Angelos waded in and slung a punch at the offender. With a menacing roar, the boy's mates rushed to the rescue. Angelos disappeared into the fray and Maxie screamed and screamed at the top of her voice in absolute panic.

'Get off him!' she shrieked, laying about the squirming clutch of heaving bodies with vicious jabs of her umbrella and her feet as well.

Simultaneously a noisy crowd came out of the pub across the street and just as suddenly the scrum broke and scattered. Maxie knelt down on the wet pavement beside Angelos's prone body and pushed his curling wet black hair off his brow, noting the pallor of his dark skin. 'You stupid fool…you stupid, stupid fool,' she moaned shakily.

Angelos lifted his head and shook it in a rather jerky movement. Slowly he began to pick himself up. Blood was running down his temples. 'There were five of them,' he grated, with clenched and bruised fists.

'Get in your car and shut up in case they come back,' Maxie muttered, tugging suggestively at his arm. 'Other people don't want to get involved these days. You could've been hammered to a pulp—'

'*Them and who else?*' Angelos flared explosively, all male ego and fireworks.

'The police station is just down the street—'

'I'm not going to the police over the head of those little punks!' Angelos snarled, staggering slightly and spreading his long powerful legs to steady himself. 'I got in a punch or two of my own—'

'Not as many as they did.' Maxie hauled at his sleeve and by dint of sustained pressure nudged him round to the passenger side of his opulent sports car.

'What are you doing?'

'You're not fit to drive—'

'Since when?' he interrupted in disbelief.

Maxie yanked open the door. 'Please, Angelos…you're bleeding, you're probably concussed. Just for once in your wretched life, do as someone else asks.'

He stood there and thought about that stunning concept for a whole twenty seconds. There was a definite struggle taking place and then, with a muffled curse, he gradually and stiffly lowered himself down into the passenger seat.

'Can you drive a Ferrari?' he enquired.

'Of course,' Maxie responded between clenched teeth of determination, no better than him at backing down.

The Ferrari lurched and jerked up the road.

'Lights,' Angelos muttered weakly. 'I think you should have the lights on…or maybe I should just close my eyes—'

'Shut up…I'm trying to concentrate!'

Having mastered the lights and located the right gear, Maxie continued, 'It was typical of you to go leaping in, fists flying. Where are your security guards, for goodness' sake?'

'How *dare* you?' Angelos splintered, leaning forward with an outrage somewhat tempered by the groan he emitted as the seat belt forced him to rest back again. 'I can look after myself—'

'Against five of them?' Maxie's strained mouth compressed, her stomach still curdling at what she had witnessed. Damn him, damn him. She felt so horribly guilty and shaken. 'I'm taking you to Casualty—'

'I don't need a doctor…I'm OK,' Angelos bit out in exasperation.

'If you drop dead from a skull fracture or something,' she said grimly, 'I don't want to feel responsible!'

'I have cuts and bruises, nothing more. I have no need

of a hospital. All I want to do is lie down for a while and then I'll call for a car.'

He sounded more like himself. Domineering and organised. Maxie mulled over that unspoken demand for a place to lie down while she crept along the road in the direction of the cottage at the slowest speed a Ferrari had probably ever been driven at. Then the heavy rain was bouncing off the windscreen and visibility was poor. 'All right...I'll take you home with me—but just for an hour,' she warned tautly.

'You are so gracious.'

Maxie reddened, conscience-stricken when she recalled the amount of trouble he had taken to ensure that she was properly looked after when she was ill. But then Angelos had not been personally inconvenienced; he had paid others to take on the caring role. In fact, as she drove up the lane to the cottage, she knew she could not imagine Angelos allowing himself to be inconvenienced.

Her attention distracted, she was wholly unprepared to find herself driving through rippling water as she began to turn in at the front of the cottage. In alarm, she braked sharply, and without warning the powerful car went into a skid. 'Oh, God!' she gasped in horror as the front wheels went over the edge of the stream bank. The Ferrari tipped into the stream nose-first with a jarring thud and came to rest at an extreme angle.

'God wasn't listening, but at least we're still alive,' Angelos groaned as he reached over and switched off the engine.

'I suppose you're about to kick up a whole macho fuss now, and yap about women drivers,' Maxie hissed, unclamping her locked fingers from the steering wheel.

'I wouldn't dare. Knowing my luck in your radius, I'd step out of the car and drown.'

'The stream is only a couple of feet deep!'

'I feel so comforted knowing that.' With a powerful

thrust of his arm, Angelos forced the passenger door open and staggered out onto the muddy bank. Then he reached in to haul her out with stunning strength.

'I'm sorry... I got a fright when I saw that water.'

'It was only a large puddle. What do you do when you see the sea?'

'I thought the stream had flooded and broken its banks, and I wanted to be sure we didn't go over the edge in the dark...that's *why* I jumped on the brakes!' Fumbling for her key, not wishing to dwell on quite how unsuccessful her evasive tactics had been, Maxie unlocked the battered front door and switched on the light.

Angelos lowered his wildly tousled dark head to peer, unimpressed, into the bare lounge with its two seater hard-backed settee. Without the fire lit or a decorative face-lift, it didn't look very welcoming, she had to admit.

'All right, upstairs is a bit more comfortable. You can lie down on my bed.'

'I can hardly believe your generosity. Where's the phone?'

Maxie frowned. 'I don't have one.'

Tangled wet black lashes swept up on stunned eyes. 'That's a joke?'

'Surely you have a mobile phone?'

'I must've dropped it in the street during the fight.' With a mutter of frustrated Greek, Angelos started up the narrow staircase.

He was a little unsteady on his feet, and Maxie noted that fact anxiously. 'I think you need a doctor, Angelos.'

'Rubbish...just want to lie down—'

'Duck your head!' she warned a split second too late as he collided headfirst with the lintel above the bedroom door.

'Oh, no,' Maxie groaned in concert with him, and shot out both arms to support him as he reeled rather danger-ously on the tiny landing. Hurriedly she guided him into the bedroom before he could do any further damage to himself.

'There's puddles on the floor,' Angelos remarked, blinking rapidly.

'Don't be silly,' Maxie told him, just as a big drop of water from somewhere above splashed down on her nose.

Aghast, she tipped back her head to gaze up at the vaulted wooden roof above, which she had thought was so much more attractive and unusual than a ceiling. Droplets of water were suspended in several places and there *were* puddles on the floorboards. The roof was leaking.

'I'm in the little hovel in the woods,' Angelos framed.

Maxie said a most unladylike word and darted over to the bed to check that it wasn't wet. Mercifully it appeared to be occupying the only dry corner in the room, but she wrenched back the bedding to double-check. Angelos dropped down on the edge of the divan and tugged off his jacket. It fell in a puddle. She snatched up the garment and clutched it as she met dazed black eyes. 'I shouldn't have listened you. I should've taken you to Casualty.'

'I have a very sore head and I am slightly disorientated. That is *all*.' Angelos coined the assurance with arrogant emphasis. 'Stop treating me like a child.'

'How many fingers do you see?' In her anxiety, Maxie stuck out her thumb instead of the forefinger she had intended.

'I see one thumb,' he said very drily. 'Was that a trick question?'

Flushing a deep pink, Maxie bridled as he yanked off his tie. 'Do you have to undress?'

'I am not lying down in wet clothes,' Angelos informed her loftily.

'I'll leave you, then…well, I need to get some bowls for the drips anyway,' Maxie mumbled awkwardly on her passage out through the door.

Just the thought of Angelos unclothed shot a shocking

current of snaking heat right through her trembling body. It was only nervous tension, Maxie told herself urgently as she went downstairs, the result of delayed shock after that horrendous outbreak of masculine violence in the street. *She* had been really scared, but Angelos was too bone-deep macho and stupid to have been scared. However, she should have forced him to go to the local hospital...but how did you force a male as spectacularly stubborn as Angelos to do something he didn't want to do, and surely there couldn't be anything really serious wrong with him when he could still be so sarcastic?

In the scullery, she picked up a bucket and a mop, and then abandoned them to pour some disinfectant into a bowl of water instead. She needed to see close up how bad that cut was. Had he been unconscious for several seconds after the youths had run off? His eyes had been closed, those ridiculously long lashes down like black silk fans and almost hitting his cheekbones. Dear heaven, what was the matter with her? Her mind didn't feel like her own any more.

Angelos was under her rosebud-sprigged sheets when she hesitantly entered the bedroom again. His eyes seemed closed. She moistened her lower lip with a nervous flick of her tongue. She took in the blatant virility of his big brown shoulders, the rough black curls of hair sprinkling what she could see of his powerful pectoral muscles and that vibrant golden skintone that seemed to cover all of him, and which looked so noticeable against her pale bedding...

'You're supposed to stay awake if you have concussion,' she scolded sharply in response to those unnecessarily intimate observations. Stepping close to the bed, she jabbed at a big brown shoulder and swiftly withdrew her hand from the heat of him again as if she had been scalded, her fair skin burning.

Those amazing black eyes snapped open on her.

'You're bleeding all over my pillow,' Maxie censured, her throat constricting as she ran completely out of breath.

'I'll buy you a new one.'

'No, you buy nothing for me...and you lie still,' she instructed unevenly. 'I need to see that cut.'

With an embarrassingly unsteady hand and a pad of kitchen towelling, Maxie cleaned away the blood. As she exposed the small seeping wound, a beautifully shaped brown hand lifted and closed round the delicate bones of her wrist. 'You're shaking like a leaf.'

'You might've been knifed or something. I still feel sick thinking about it. But I could've dealt with that kid on my own—'

'I think not...his mates were already moving in to have some fun. Nor would it have cost them much effort to drag you round the corner down that alleyway—'

'Well, I'm not about to thank you. If you had stayed away from me, it wouldn't have happened,' Maxie stated tightly. 'I'd have stayed in the hotel until closing time and got a lift home with the barman. He lives a couple of miles on down the road.'

With that final censorious declaration, Maxie pulled herself free and took the bowl downstairs again. She would have to go back up and mop the floor but it was true, she *was* shaking like a leaf and her legs felt like jelly. Unfortunately it wasn't all the result of shock. Seeing Angelos in her bed, wondering like a nervous adolescent how much, if anything, he was wearing, hadn't helped.

Five minutes later she went back up, with a motley collection of containers to catch the drips and the mop and bucket. In silence, she did what had to be done, but she was horribly mortified by the necessity, not to mention furious with herself for dismissing the agent's assessment of the cottage's condition on the phone. This was the first time it had rained since she had moved in and clearly either a new roof or substantial repairs would be required to make the cottage waterproof before winter set in. It was doubtful that she could afford even repairs.

As each receptacle was finally correctly positioned to catch the drips from overhead, a cacophany of differing noises started up. Split, splat, splash, plop...

'How are you feeling?' Maxie asked thinly above that intrusive backdrop of constant drips.

'Fantastically rich and spoilt. Indoors, water belongs in the bathroom or the swimming pool,' Angelos opined with sardonic cool. 'I can't credit that you would prefer to risk drowning under a roof that leaks like a sieve sooner than come to me.'

'Credit it. Nothing you could do or say would convince me otherwise. I don't want to live with any man—'

'I wasn't actually asking you to live with me,' Angelos delivered in gentle contradiction, his sensual mouth quirking. 'I like my own space. I would buy you your own place and visit—'

An angry flush chased Maxie's strained pallor. 'I'm not for sale—'

'Except for a wedding ring?' Angelos vented a roughened laugh of cynical amusement. 'Oh, yes, I got the message. Very naive, but daring. I may be obsessed with a need to possess that exquisite body that trembles with sexual hunger whenever I am close,' he murmured silkily, reaching up with a confident hand to close his fingers over hers and draw her down beside him before she even registered what he was doing, 'but, while I will fulfil any other desire or ambition with pleasure, that one is out of reach, *pethi mou*. Concentrate on the possible, not the wildly improbable.'

'If you didn't already have a head injury, I'd swing for you!' Maxie slung fiercely. 'Let go of me!'

In the controlled and easy gesture of a very strong male, Angelos released her with a wry smile. 'At the end of the day, Leland did quite a number on your confidence, didn't he? Oh, yes, I know that *he* dispatched *you* from the hospital and screeched for Jennifer. Suddenly you found yourself back on the street, alone and without funds. So I quite understand why you should decide that a husband would be a safer bet than a lover next time around. However, I am *not* Leland...'

Maxie stared down into those stunning dark golden eyes. Fear and fascination fought for supremacy inside her. She could feel the raw magnetism of him reaching out to entrap her and she knew her own weakness more and more with every passing second in his company. She hated him but she wanted him too, with a bone-deep yearning for physical contact that tormented her this close to him. She was appalled by the strength of his sexual sway over her, shattered that she could be so treacherously vulnerable with a male of his ilk.

'Come here...stop holding back,' Angelos urged softly. 'Neither of us can win a battle like this. Do we not both suffer? I faithfully promise that I will never, ever take advantage of you as Leland did—'

'What are you trying to do right now?' Maxie condemned strickenly.

'Trying to persuade you that trusting me would be in your best interests. And I'm not laying a finger on you,' Angelos added, as if he expected acclaim for that remarkable restraint.

And the terrible irony, she registered then, was that she *wanted* him to touch her. Her bright eyes pools of sapphire-blue dismay and hunger, she stared down at him. Reaching up to loosen the band confining her hair to the nape of her neck, Angelos trailed it gently free to wind long brown fingers into the tumbling strands and slowly tug her down to him.

'But that's not what you want either, is it?' he said perceptively.

'No...' Her skin burning beneath the caress of the blunt

forefinger that skated along her tremulous and full lower lip, she shivered violently. 'But I won't give in. This attraction means nothing to me,' she swore raggedly. 'It won't influence my brain—'

'What a heady challenge...' Black eyes flaring with golden heat held her sensually bemused gaze.

'I'm not a challenge, I'm a woman...' Maxie fumbled in desperation to make her feelings clear but she didn't have the words or, it seemed, the self-discipline to pull back from his embrace.

'A hell of a woman, to fight me like this,' Angelos confirmed, with a thickened appreciation that made her heart pound like mad in her eardrums and a tide of disorientating dizziness enclose her. 'A woman worth fighting for. If you could just rise above this current inconvenient desire to turn over a new leaf—'

'But—'

'No buts.' Angelos leant up to brush his lips in subtle glancing punishment over her parted ones, scanning her with fierce sexual hunger and conviction. 'You *need* me.'

'No...' she whispered feverishly.

'*Yes*...' Dipping his tongue in a snaking explorative flick into her open mouth, Angelos jolted her with such an overpowering stab of excitement, she almost collapsed down on top of him.

Pressing his advantage with a ruthless sense of timing, Angelos tumbled her the rest of the way and gathered her into his arms. She gasped again, 'No.'

The palm curving over a pouting, swollen breast stilled. Her nipple was a hard, straining bud that ached and begged for his attention, and she let her swimming head drop down on the pillow while she fought desperately for control. She focused on him. The brilliant eyes, the strong nose, the ruthless mouth. And that appalling tide of painful craving simply mushroomed instead of fading.

'No?' Angelos queried lazily.

She inched forward like a moth to a candle flame, seeking the heat and virility she could not resist, all thought suspended. He recognised surrender when he saw it, and with a wolfish smile of reward he closed his mouth hungrily over hers and she burned up like a shooting star streaking through the heavens at impossible speed, embracing destruction as if she had been born to seek it.

He curved back from her when her every sense was thrumming unbearably, her whole body shaking on a peak of frantic anticipation, and eased one hand beneath the T-shirt to curve it to her bare breasts. She whimpered and jerked, the most terrifying surge of hunger taking over as his expert fingers tugged on her tender nipples and then his caressing mouth went there instead. For long, timeless minutes, Maxie was a shuddering wreck of writhing, gasping response, clutching at him, clutching at his hair, her denim-clad hips rising off the bed in helpless invitation.

Abruptly Angelos tensed and jerked up his dark head, frowning. 'What's that?' he demanded.

'W-what's what?' she stammered blankly.

'Someone's thumping on the front door.'

By then already engaged in gaping down at her own shamelessly bared breasts, the damp evidence of his carnal ministrations making the distended pink buds look even more wanton, Maxie gulped. With a low moan of distress she threw herself off the bed onto quaking legs.

'You swine,' she accused shakily, hauling down her T-shirt, crossing trembling arms and then rushing for the stairs.

She flung open the front door. Her nearest neighbour, Patrick Devenson, who had called in to introduce himself the day before, stared in at her. 'Are you aware that you have a Ferrari upended in your stream?'

Dumbly, still trembling from the narrowness of her escape from Angelos and his seductive wiles, Maxie nodded like a wooden marionette.

The husky blond veterinary surgeon frowned down at her. 'I was driving home and I saw this strange shape from the road, and, knowing you're on your own here, I thought I'd better check it out. Are you OK?'

'The driver's upstairs, lying down,' Maxie managed to say.

'Want me to take a look?'

'No need,' she hastened to assert breathlessly.

'Do you want me to ring a doctor?'

Maxie focused on the mobile in its holder at his waist. 'I'd be terribly grateful if you'd let me use that to make a call.'

'No problem...' Patrick said easily, and passed the phone over. 'Mind if I step in out of the rain?'

'Sorry, not at all.'

Maxie walked upstairs rigid-backed, crossed the room and plonked the phone down on the bed beside Angelos. 'Call for transport out of here or I'll throw you out in the rain!'

His stunningly handsome features froze into impassivity, but not before she saw the wild burn of outrage flare in the depths of his brilliant eyes. He stabbed the buttons, loosed a flood of bitten-out Greek instructions and then, cutting the connection, sprang instantly out of bed. Maddeningly, he swayed slightly.

But Maxie was less affected by that than by her first intimidating look at a naked and very aroused male. Colouring hotly, she dragged her shaken scrutiny from him and fled downstairs again.

'Thanks,' she told Patrick.

'Had a drink or two, had he? Wicked putting a machine like that in for a swim,' Patrick remarked with typical male superiority as he moved very slowly back to the door. 'Your boyfriend?'

'No, he's not.'

'Dinner with me then, tomorrow night?'

Words of automatic refusal brimmed on Maxie's lips, and then she hesitated. 'Why not?' she responded after that brief pause for thought. She was well aware that Angelos had to be hearing every word of the conversation.

'Wonderful!' Patrick breathed with unconcealed pleasure. 'Eight suit you?'

'Lovely.'

She watched him swing cheerfully back into his four-wheel drive and thought about how open and uncomplicated he was in comparison to Angelos, who was so devious and manipulative he would contrive to zigzag down a perfectly straight line. And she hated Angelos, she really did.

Hot tears stung her eyes then, and she blinked them back furiously. She hated him for showing her all over again how weak and foolish she could be. She hated that cool, clever brain he pitted against her, that brilliantly persuasive tongue that could make the unacceptable sound tempting, and that awesome and terrifying sexual heat he unleashed on her whenever she was vulnerable.

Barely five minutes later, Angelos strode fully dressed into the front room where she was waiting. He radiated black fury, stormy eyes glittering, sensual mouth compressed, rock-hard jawline at an aggressive angle. His hostile vibrations lanced through the already tense atmosphere, threatening to set it on fire.

'You bitch...' Angelos breathed, so hoarsely it sounded as if he could hardly get the words out. 'One minute you're in bed with me and the next you're making a date with another man within my hearing!'

'I wasn't in bed with you, not the way you're implying.' Her slender hands knotted into taut fists of determination by her side, Maxie stood her ground, cringing with angry self-loathing only inside herself.

'You don't *want* any other man!' Angelos launched at her with derisive and shocking candour. 'You want *me*!'

Maxie was bone-white, her knees wobbling. In a rage, Angelos was pure intimidation; there was nothing he would not say. 'I won't be your mistress. I made that clear that from the start,' she countered in a ragged rush. 'And even if I had slept with you just now, I would still have asked you to leave. I will not be cajoled, manipulated or seduced into a relationship that I would find degrading—'

'Only an innocent can be seduced.' His accent harshened with incredulity over that particular choice of word. *'Degrading?'* Outrage clenched his vibrant dark features hard. 'Fool that I am, I would have treated you like a precious jewel!'

Locked up tight somewhere, to be enjoyed only in the strictest privacy, Maxie translated, deeply unimpressed.

'I know you don't believe me, but I was never Leland's mistress—'

'Did you call yourself his lover instead?' Angelos derided.

Maxie swallowed convulsively. 'No, I—'

Grim black eyes clashed with hers in near physical assault. *'Theos*...how blind I have been! All along you've been scheming to extract a better offer from me. One step forward, two steps back. You run and I chase. You tease and I pursue,' he enumerated in harsh condemnation. 'And now you're trying to turn the screw by playing me off against another man—'

'No!' Maxie gasped, unnerved by the twisted light he saw her in.

Angelos growled, 'If you think for one second that you can force me to offer a wedding ring for the right to enjoy that beautiful body, you are certifiably insane!'

His look of unconcealed contempt sent scorching anger tearing through Maxie. 'Really...? Well, isn't that just a shame, when it's the only offer I would ever settle for,' she stated, ready to use any weapon to hold him at bay.

Evidently somewhat stunned to have his worst suspicions

so baldly confirmed, Angelos jerked as if he had run into a brick wall. He snatched in a shuddering breath, his nostrils flaring. 'If I ever marry, my wife will be a lady with breeding, background and a decent reputation.'

Maxie flinched, stomach turning over sickly. She had given him a knife and he had plunged it in without compunction. But ferocious pride as great as his own, and hot, violent loathing enabled her to treat him to a scornful appraisal. 'But you'll still have a mistress, won't you?'

'Naturally I would choose a wife with my brain, not my libido,' Angelos returned drily, but he had ducked the question and a dark, angry rise of blood had scoured his blunt cheekbones.

Maxie gave an exaggerated little shiver of revulsion. The atmosphere was explosive. She could feel his struggle to maintain control over that volatile temperament so much at war with that essentially cool intellect of his. It was etched in every restive, powerfully physical movement he made with his expressive hands and she rejoiced at the awareness, ramming down the stark bitterness and sense of pained inadequacy he had filled her with. 'You belong in the Natural History Museum alongside the dinosaur bones.'

'When I walk through that door I will never come back...how will you like that?'

'Would you like to start walking now?'

'What I would *like* is to take you on that bed upstairs and teach you just once exactly what you're missing!'

Wildly unprepared for that roughened admission, Maxie collided with golden eyes ablaze with frustration. It was like being dragged into a fire and burned by her own hunger. She shivered convulsively. 'Dream on,' she advised fiercely, but her voice shook in self-betrayal.

The noise of a car drawing up outside broke the taut silence.

Angelos inclined his arrogant dark head in a gesture of grim dismissal that made her squirm, and then he walked.

CHAPTER SIX

MAXIE drifted like a sleepwalker through the following five days. The Ferrari was retrieved by a tow-truck and two men who laughed like drains throughout the operation. She contacted a builder to have the roof inspected and the news was as bad as she had feared. The cottage needed to be reroofed, and the quote was way beyond her slender resources.

She dined out with Patrick Devenson. No woman had ever tried harder to be attracted to a man. He was good-looking and easy company. Desperate to feel a spark, she let him kiss her at the end of the evening, but it wasn't like falling on an electric fence, it was like putting on a pair of slippers. Seriously depressed, Maxie made an excuse when he asked when he could see her again.

She didn't sleep, *couldn't* sleep. She dreamt of fighting with Angelos. She dreamt of making wild, passionate love for the first time in her life. And, most grotesque of all, she dreamt of drifting down a church aisle towards a scowling, struggling Greek in handcuffs. She felt like an alien inside her own head and body.

She sat down and painstakingly made a list of every flaw that Angelos possessed. It covered two pages. In a rage with herself, she wept over that list. She loathed him. Yet that utterly mindless craving for his enlivening, domineering Neanderthal man presence persisted, killing her appetite and depriving her of all peace of mind.

How could she miss him, how could she possibly? How *could* simple sexual attraction be so devastating a leveller? she asked herself in furious despair and shame. And, since she could only be suffering from the fallout of having repressed her own physical needs for so long, why on earth hadn't she fancied Patrick?

At lunchtime on the fifth day, she heard a car coming up the lane and went to the window. A silver Porsche pulled up. When Catriona Ferguson emerged, Maxie was startled. She had never in her life qualified for a personal visit from the owner of the Star modelling agency and couldn't begin to imagine what could've brought the spiky, city-loving redhead all the way from town.

On the doorstep, Catriona dealt her a wide, appreciative smile. 'I've got to hand it to you, Maxie…you have to be the Comeback Queen of the Century.'

'You've got some work for me?' Maxie ushered her visitor into the front room.

'Since the rumour mill got busy, you're really *hot*,' Catriona announced with satisfaction. 'The day after tomorrow, there's a Di Venci fashion show being staged in London…a big splashy charity do, and your chance to finally make your debut on the couture circuit.'

'The rumour mill?' Maxie was stunned by what the older woman was telling her. One minute she was yesterday's news and the next she was being offered the biggest break of her career to date? That didn't make sense.

Having sat down to open a tiny electronic notepad, Catriona flashed her an amused glance. 'The gossip columns are rumbling like mad…don't you read your own publicity?'

Maxie stiffened. 'I don't buy newspapers.'

'I'm very discreet. Your private life is your own.' However, Catriona still searched Maxie's face with avid curiosity. 'But what a coup for a lady down on her luck, scandalously maligned and dropped into social obscurity… Only one of the richest men in the world—'

Maxie jerked. 'I don't know what you're talking about.'

Catriona raised pencilled brows. 'I'm only talking about the guy who has just single-handedly relaunched your career without knowing it! The paparazzo who had his film exposed howled all over the tabloids about who he had seen you with—'

'You're talking about Angelos...'

'And when I received a cautious visit from a tight-mouthed gentleman I know to be close to the Greek tycoon himself, I was just totally *amazed*, not to mention impressed to death,' Catriona trilled, her excitement unconcealed. 'So I handed over your address. They say Angelos Petronides never forgets a favour...or, for that matter, a slight.'

Maxie had turned very pale. 'I...'

'So why are you up here vegetating next door to a field of sheep?' Catriona angled a questioning glance at her. 'Treat 'em mean, keep 'em keen? Popular report has it that this very week he dumped Natalie Cibaud for you. Whatever you're doing would appear to be working well. And he's an awesome catch, twenty-two-carat gorgeous, and as for that delicious *scary* reputation of his—'

'There's nothing between Angelos and me,' Maxie cut in with flat finality, but her head buzzed with the information that Angelos had evidently still been seeing the glamorous French film actress.

The silence that fell was sharp.

'If it's already over, keep it to yourself.' Catriona's disappointment was blatant. 'The sudden clamour for your services relates very much to *him*. The story that you've captured his interest is enough to raise you to celebrity status right now. So keep the people guessing for as long as you can...'

When Maxie recalled how appalled she had been at the threat of being captured in newsprint with Angelos and being subjected to more lurid publicity, she very nearly choked at that cynical advice. And when she considered how outraged Angelos must be at the existence of such rumours, when he had demanded her discretion, she sucked in a sustaining breath.

Catriona checked her watch. 'Look, why don't I give you a lift back to town? I suggest you stay with that friend in the suburbs again. The paparazzi are scouring the pavements for you. You don't want to be found yet. You need to make the biggest possible impact when you appear on that catwalk.'

It took guts, but Maxie nodded agreement. The old story, she thought bitterly. She needed the money. Not just for the roof but also to pay off Angelos as well. Yet the prospect of all those flashing cameras and the vitriolic pens of the gossip columnists made her sensitive stomach churn. Money might not buy happiness, but the lack of it could destroy all freedom of choice. And Maxie acknowledged then that the precious freedom to choose her own way of life was what she now craved most.

Scanning Maxie's strained face, Catriona sighed. 'Whatever *has* happened to the Ice Queen image?'

As she packed upstairs, Maxie knew the answer to that. Angelos had happened. He had chipped her out from behind the safety of her cool, unemotional façade by making her feel things she had never felt before...painful things, hurtful things. She wanted the ice back far more desperately than Catriona did.

Maxie came off the catwalk to a rousing bout of thunderous applause. Immediately she abandoned the strutting insolent carriage which was playing merry hell with her backbone. Finished, *at last*. The relief was so huge, she trembled. Never in her life had she felt so exposed.

Before she could reach the changing room, Manny Di Venci, a big bruiser of a man with a shaven head and sharp eyes, came backstage to intercept her. 'You were brilliant! Standing room only out there, but now it's time to beat a fast retreat. No, you don't need to get changed,' the designer laughed, urging her at a fast pace down a dimly lit corridor that disorientated her even more after the glaring spotlights of the show. 'You're the best PR my collection has ever had, and a special lunch-date demands a touch of Di Venci class.'

Presumably Catriona had set up lunch with some VIP she had to impress.

Thrust through a rear entrance onto a pavement drenched in sunlight, Maxie was dazzled again. Squinting at the open door of the waiting vehicle, she climbed in. The car had pulled back into the traffic before she registered that she was in a huge, opulent limo with shaded windows, but she relaxed when she saw the huge squashy bag of her possessions sitting on the floor. She checked the bag; her clothes were in it too. Somebody had been very efficient.

Off the catwalk, she was uncomfortable in the daring peacock-blue cocktail suit. She wore only skin below the fitted jacket with its plunging neckline, and the skirt was horrendously tight and short. She would have preferred not to meet a potential client in so revealing an outfit, but she might as well make the best of being sought after while it lasted because it wouldn't last long. The minute Angelos appeared in public with another woman, she would be as 'hot' as a cold potato. But oh, how infuriating it must be for Angelos to have played an accidental part in pushing her back into the limelight!

When the door of the limo swung open, Maxie stepped out into a cold, empty basement car park. She froze in astonishment, attacked by sudden mute terror, and then across the vast echoing space she recognised one of Angelos's security men, and was insensibly relieved for all of ten seconds. But the nightmare image of kidnapping which had briefly gripped her was immediately replaced by a sensation of almost suffocating panic.

'Where am I?' she demanded of the older man standing by a lift with the doors wide in readiness.

'Mr Petronides is waiting for you on the top floor, Miss Kendall.'

'I didn't realise that limo was *his*. I thought I was meeting up with my agent and a client for lunch…this is o-outrageous!' Hearing the positively pathetic shake of rampant nerves in her own voice, Maxie bit her lip and stalked into the lift. She was furious with herself. She had been the one to make assumptions. She should have spoken to the chauffeur before she got into the car.

Like a protective wall in front of her, the security man stayed by the doors, standing back again only after they had opened. Her face taut with temper, Maxie walked out into a big octagonal hall with a cool tiled floor. It was not Angelos's apartment and she frowned, wondering where on earth she was. Behind her the lift whirred downward again and she stiffened, feeling ludicrously cut off from escape.

Ahead of her, a door stood wide. She walked into a spacious, luxurious reception room. Strong sunlight was pouring through the windows. The far end of the room seemed to merge into a lush green bank of plants. Patio doors gave way into what appeared to be a conservatory. Was that where Angelos was waiting for her?

Her heart hammered wildly against her ribs. Utterly despising her own undeniable mix of apprehension and excitement, Maxie threw back her slim shoulders and stalked out into…*fresh air*. Too late did she appreciate that she was actually out on a roof garden. As she caught a dizzy glimpse of the horrific drop through a gap in the decorative stone screening to her right, her head reeled. Freezing to the spot, she uttered a sick moan of fear.

'Oh, hell…you're afraid of heights,' a lazy drawl murmured.

A pair of hands closed with firm reassurance round her whip-taut shoulders and eased her back from the parapet and the view that had made her stomach lurch to her soles. 'I didn't think of that. Though I suppose I could keep you standing out here and persuade you to agree to just about anything. Sometimes it's *such* a challenge to be an honourable man.'

Shielding her from the source of her mindless terror with his big powerful frame, Angelos propelled her back indoors at speed. Appalled by the attack of panic which had thrown her off balance, Maxie broke free of him then, on legs shaking like cotton wool pins, and bit out accusingly, 'What would *you* know about honour?'

'The Greek male can be extremely sensitive on that subject. Think before you speak,' Angelos murmured in chilling warning.

Maxie stared at him in surprise. Angelos stared levelly back at her, black eyes terrifyingly cold.

And it tore her apart just at that moment to learn that she couldn't *bear* him to look at her like that. As if she was just anybody, as if she was nobody, as if he didn't care whether she lived or died.

'You get more nervy every time I see you,' Angelos remarked with cruel candour. 'Paler, thinner too. I thought you were pretty tough, but you're not so tough under sustained pressure. Your stress level is beginning to show.'

Colour sprang into Maxie's cheeks, highlighting the feverish look in her gaze. 'You're such a bastard sometimes,' she breathed unevenly.

'And within itself, that's strange. I've never been like this with a woman before. There are times when I aim to hurt you and I shock myself,' Angelos confided, without any perceptible remorse.

Yet he still looked so unbelievably good to her, and that terrified her. She couldn't drag her attention from that lean, strong face, no matter how hard she tried. She couldn't forget what that silky black hair had felt like beneath her fingertips. She couldn't stop herself noticing that he was wearing what had inexplicably become the colour she liked best on him. Silver-grey, the suit a spectacular fit for that magnificent physique. And how had she forgotten the way that vibrant aura of raw energy compelled and fascinated her? Cast into deeper shock by the raging torrent of her own frantic thoughts, Maxie felt an intense sense of her own vulnerability engulf her in an alarming wave.

'Relax…I've got a decent proposal to put on the table before lunch,' Angelos purred, strolling soundlessly forwards to curve a confident arm round her rigid spine and guide her across the hall into a dining-room. 'Trust me…I think you'll feel like you've won the National Lottery.'

'Why won't you just leave me alone?' Maxie whispered, taking in the table exquisitely set for two, the waiting trolley that indicated they were not to be disturbed.

'Because you don't want me to. Even the way you just looked at me…' Angelos vented a soft husky laugh of very masculine appreciation. 'You really *can't* look at me like that and expect me to throw in the towel.'

'How did I look?'

'Probably much the same way that I look at you,' he conceded, uncorking a bottle of champagne with a loud pop and allowing the golden liquid to foam expertly down into two fluted glasses. 'With hunger and hostility and resentment. I am about to wipe out the last two for ever.'

Angelos slotted the moisture-beaded glass between her taut fingers. Absorbing her incomprehension, he dealt her a slashing smile. 'The rumour that Angelos Petronides cannot compromise is a complete falsehood. I excell at seeing both points of view and a period of reflection soon clarified the entire problem. The solution is very simple.'

Maxie frowned uneasily. 'I don't know what you're driving at…'

'What *is* marriage? Solely a legal agreement.' Angelos shrugged with careless elegance but she was chilled by that definition. 'Once I recognised that basic truth, I saw with clarity. I'll make a deal with you now that suits us both. *You* sign a prenuptial contract and I *will* marry you…'

'S-say that again,' Maxie stammered, convinced she was hallucinating.

Angelos rested satisfied eyes on her stunned expression. 'The one drawback will be that you won't get the public kudos of being my wife. We will live apart much of the time. When I'm in London and I want you here, you will stay in this apartment. I own this entire building. You can have it all to yourself, complete with a full complement of staff and security. The only place we will share the same roof will be on my island in Greece. How am I doing?'

Maxie's hand was shaking so badly, champagne was slopping onto the thick, ankle-deep carpet. Was he actually asking her to marry him? Had she got that right or imagined it? And, if she was correct and hadn't misunderstood, why was he talking about them living apart? And what had that bit been concerning 'public kudos'? Her brain was in a hopelessly confused state of freefall.

Angelos took her glass away and set it aside with his own. He pressed her gently down onto the sofa behind her and crouched down at her level to scan her bewildered face.

'If a marriage licence is what it takes to make you feel secure and bring you to my bed, it would be petty to deny you,' Angelos informed her smoothly. 'But, since our relationship will obviously not last for ever, it will be a private arrangement between you and I alone.'

Maxie stopped breathing and simply closed her eyes. He had hurt her before but never as badly as this. Was her reputation really *that* bad? In his eyes, it evidently was, she registered sickly. He didn't want to be seen with her. He didn't want to be linked with her. He would go through the motions of marrying her only so long as it was a 'private arrangement'. And a temporary one.

Cool, strong hands snapped round her straining fingers as she began to move them in an effort to jump upright. 'No…think about it, don't fly off the handle,' Angelos warned steadily. 'It's a fair, realistic, what-you-see-is-what-you-get offer—'

'A mockery!' Maxie contradicted fiercely.

And that had to be the most awful moment imaginable to realise that she was very probably in love with Angelos. It was without doubt her lowest hour. Devastated to suspect just how and why he had come to possess this power to tear her to emotional shreds, Maxie was shorn of her usual fire.

'Be reasonable. How do I bring Leland's former mistress into my family and demand that they accept her as my wife?' Angelos enquired with the disorientating cool of someone saying the most reasonable, rational things and expecting a fair and understanding hearing. 'Some things one just does not do. How can I expect my family to respect me if I do something I would kill any one of them for doing? The family look to me to set an example.'

Maxie still hadn't opened her eyes, but she knew at that instant how a woman went off the rails and killed. There was so much pain inside her and so much rage—at her, at him—she didn't honestly know how she *could* contain it. Mistress within a marriage that nobody would ever know about because she was too scandalous and shameful a woman to deserve or indeed expect acceptance within the lofty Petronides clan...that was what he was offering.

'I feel sick...' Maxie muttered raggedly.

'No, you do not feel sick,' Angelos informed her with resolute emphasis.

'I...feel...sick!'

'The cloakroom is across the hall.' Angelos withdrew his strong hands from hers in a stark demonstration of disapproval. Only when he did so did she realise how tightly she had been holding onto him for support. The inconsistency of such behaviour in the midst of so devastating a dialogue appalled her. 'I didn't expect you to be so difficult about this. I can appreciate that you're a little disappointed with the boundaries I'm setting, but when all is said and done, it is *still* a marriage proposal!'

'Is it?' Maxie queried involuntarily, and then, not trusting herself to say anything more, she finally, mercifully made it into the sanctuary of the cloakroom.

She locked the door and lurched in front of a giant mirror that reflected a frightening stranger with the shocked staring eyes of tragedy, pallid cheeks and a horribly wobbly mouth. You do *not* love that swine—do you hear me? she mouthed with menace at the alien weak creature in the reflection. The only thing you're in love with is his *body*! She knew as much about love as a fourteen-year-old with a crush! And she could not imagine where that insane impulsive idea that she might love such a unreconstructed pig could've come from…it could only have been a reaction to overwhelming shock.

She wanted to scream and cry and break things and she knew she couldn't, so she hugged herself tight instead and paced the floor. As there was a great deal of floor available, in spite of the fact it was only a cloakroom, that was not a problem.

He's prepared to give you a whole blasted building to yourself. But then he does like his own space. He's prepared to do virtually anything to get you into bed except own up to you in public. Love and hate. Two sides of the same coin. A cliché but the brief, terrifying spasm of that anguished love feeling had now been wholly obliterated by loathing and a desire to hit back and hurt that was ferocious.

A *marriage* proposal? A bitter laugh erupted from Maxie. Angelos was still planning to use her, still viewing her as a live toy to be acquired at any cost for his bedroom. And evidently her reluctance had sent what he was prepared to pay for that pleasure right through the roof! Grimacing, she could not help thinking about the two men before Angelos who had most influenced her life. Her father and

Leland. For once she thought about her father without sentimentality...

Russ had gambled away her earnings and finally abandoned her, leaving her to work off *his* debts. Leland had stolen three years of her life and destroyed her reputation. How often had she sworn since never to allow any man to use her for his own ends again?

Like a bolt from the blue an infinitely more ego-boosting scenario flashed into Maxie's mind. She froze as the heady concept of turning the tables occurred to her. What if *she* were to do the using this time around?

Didn't she require a husband to inherit a share of her godmother's estate? When she had heard that news, she had taken disappointment on the chin. She had not foreseen the remotest possibility of a husband on the horizon, and the concept of looking for one with the sole object of collecting that inheritance had made her cringe.

Only no longer did Maxie feel so nice in her notions. Angelos had done that to her. He was a corrupting influence and no mistake. He had distressed her, humiliated her, harassed her, not to mention committed the ultimate sin of taking the holy bond of matrimony and twisting it into a sad, dirty joke.

Angelos saw her as an ambitious, money-grabbing bimbo without morals. No doubt he despised what he saw. He probably even despised his own obsessive hunger to possess her. The marriage, if it could be called such, wouldn't last five minutes beyond the onset of his boredom.

But what if she were to take the opportunity to turn apparent humiliation into triumph? She *could* break free of everything that had ruined her life in recent years. That debt to Angelos, a career and a life she hated, Angelos himself. If she had the courage of her convictions, she could have it *all*. Yes, she really could. She could marry him and walk out on him six months later. She pictured herself breezily throwing Angelos a cheque and telling him no, she didn't need his money, she now had her own. She looked back in the mirror and saw a killer bimbo with a brain and not a hint of tears in her eyes any more.

Maxie was surprised to find Angelos waiting in the hall when she emerged.

'Are you OK?' he enquired, as if he really cared.

Her lip wanted to curl but she controlled it. The rat. An extraordinarily handsome rat, but a rat all the same.

'I was working out my conditions of acceptance.' Maxie flashed him a bright smile of challenge.

Angelos tensed.

'I'll need to be sure I *will* feel like a Lottery winner at the end of this private arrangement,' she told him for good measure.

Angelos frowned darkly. 'My lawyer will deal with such things. Do you have to be so crude?'

Crude? My goodness, hadn't he got sensitive all of a sudden? He didn't want to be forced to dwell on the actual cost of acquiring her. And even if she didn't go for the whole package, and indeed considered herself insulted beyond belief, it *was* quite a hefty cost on his terms, Maxie conceded grudgingly. A marriage licence as the ultimate assurance of financial security—the lifestyle of a very wealthy woman and no doubt a very generous final settlement at the end of the day.

Mulling over those points, Maxie decided that he certainly couldn't accuse her of coming cheap, but she was entranced to realise that Angelos had no desire to be reminded of that unlovely fact. Just like everybody else, it seemed, Angelos Petronides preferred to believe that he was wanted for himself. She stored up that unexpected Achilles' heel for future reference.

Maxie widened her beautiful eyes at his words. 'I thought you admired the upfront approach?'

'I brought you here to celebrate a sane and sensible agreement, not to stage another argument.'

With that declaration, heated black eyes watched her flick her spectacular mane of golden hair over her slim shoulders and stayed to linger on her exquisite face. As his intent appraisal slowly arrowed down over the deep shadowy vee of her neckline, Maxie stiffened. At an almost pained pace of ever-deepening lust, his appreciative gaze wandered on down to take in the full effect of her slim hips and incredibly long legs. 'No, definitely not to have another argument,' Angelos repeated rather hoarsely.

'If your idea of celebration encompasses what I think it might, I'm afraid no can do.' Maxie swept up her glass of champagne with an apologetic smile pasted on her lips and drank deep before continuing at a fast rate of knots, 'I'll share your bed on our wedding night, but not one single second, minute, hour or day before. I suggest that we have lunch—'

'Lunch?' Angelos repeated flatly.

'We might as well do lunch because we are not about to do anything else,' Maxie informed him dulcetly.

'*Theos*...come here,' Angelos groaned. He hauled her resisting frozen length into his arms. 'Why are you always so set on punishing me?' He gave her a frustrated little shake, black eyes blazing over her mutinous expression. 'Why do you always feel the need to top everything I do and turn every encounter into a fight? That is not a womanly trait. Why cannot you just one time give me the response I expect?'

'I suppose I do it because I don't like you,' Maxie admitted, with the kind of impulsive sincerity that was indisputably convincing.

In an abrupt movement, Angelos's powerful arms dropped from her again. He actually looked shocked. 'What do you mean you don't *like* me?' he grated incredulously. 'What sort of a thing is that to say to man who has just asked you to marry him?'

'I wrote two whole pages on the subject last week...all

the things I don't like…but why should you let that bother you? You're not interested in what goes on inside my head…all you require is an available body!'

'You're overwrought, so I won't make an issue of that judgement.' Angelos frowned down into her beautiful face with the suggestion of grim self-restraint. 'Let's have lunch.'

As she sat down at the table Maxie murmured sweetly, 'One more little question. Are you planning to generously share yourself between Natalie Cibaud and me?'

Angelos glared at her for a startled second. 'Are you out of your mind?'

'That's not an answer—'

Angelos flung aside his napkin, black eyes glittering hard and bright as diamonds. 'Of course I do not intend to conduct a liaison with another woman while I am with you,' he intoned in a charged undertone.

Relaxing infinitesimally, Maxie said flatly, 'So when will the big event be taking place?'

'The wedding? As soon as possible. It will be very private.'

'I think it is so sweet that you had not a single doubt that I would say yes.' Maxie stabbed an orange segment with vicious force.

'If you want me to take you to bed to close that waspish mouth, you're going the right way.'

Looking up, Maxie clashed with gleaming black eyes full of warning. She swallowed convulsively and coloured, annoyed that she was unable to control her own fierce need to attack him.

'You told me yourself that the one offer you would settle for is marriage. I have delivered…stop using me as target practice.'

Maxie tried to eat then, but she couldn't. All appetite had ebbed, so she tried to make conversation, but it seemed rather too late for that. Angelos now exuded brooding dissatisfaction. She saw that she had already sinned. He had expected to pour a couple of glasses of champagne down her throat and sweep her triumphantly off to bed. She felt numb, for once wonderfully untouched by Angelos's incredibly powerful sexual presence.

'Are you aware that all those rumours about you and I have actually relaunched my career?' she murmured stiffly.

'Today was your swansong. I don't want you prancing down a catwalk half-naked and I don't want you working either,' Angelos framed succinctly.

'Oh,' Maxie almost whispered, because it took so much effort not to scream.

'Be sensible...naturally I want you to be available when I'm free.'

'Like a harem slave—'

'Maxie...' Angelos growled.

'Look, I've got a ripping headache,' Maxie confessed abruptly and, pushing her plate away, stood up. 'I want to go home.'

'This will be your home in London soon,' he reminded her drily.

'I don't like weird pictures and cold tiled floors and dirty great empty rooms with ugly geometric furniture...I don't want to live in a building with about ten empty floors below me!' Maxie flung, her voice rising shrilly.

'You're just overexcited—'

'Like one of your racehorses?'

With a ground-out curse, Angelos slung his napkin on the table and, thrusting his chair back, sprang to his full commanding height. As he reached for her she tried to evade him, but he simply bent and swept her up into his powerful arms and held her tight. 'Maxie...why are you suddenly behaving like a sulky child?'

'How *dare*—?'

In answer, Angelos plunged his mouth passionately hard down on hers and smashed his primal passage through every barrier. Her numbness vanished. He kissed her breathless until she was weak and trembling with tormented need in his arms. Then he looked down at her, and he stared for a very long while.

The silence unnerved her, but she was too shaken by the discovery that even a few kisses could reduce her to wanton compliance to speak.

His bronzed face utterly hard and impassive, he finally murmured flatly, 'I'll call the car for you and I'll be in touch. I don't feel like lunch now either.'

Maxie registered his distance. The sense of rejection she felt appalled her. And she thought then, If I go through with this private arrangement, if I try to play him at his own game, I will surely tear myself apart...

No—no, she wouldn't, she told herself urgently, battening down the hatches before insidious doubt could weaken her determination. One way or another she would survive with her pride intact. Wanting Angelos was solely a physical failing. Ultimately she would overcome that hunger and look forward to the life she would have *after* him.

CHAPTER SEVEN

'So, EVEN though it was a rather unconventional proposal, Angelos *did* have marriage in mind,' Liz finally sighed with satisfaction.

'Only when he saw it was his only hope.'

'I hear a lot of men are like that. Angelos is only thirty-three, but he's bound to be rather spoilt when it comes to his...well, when many other women would be willing to sleep with him without commitment,' Liz extended with warming cheeks. 'I expect you've been something of a learning experience for him, and if *you* were more sensible, he could learn a lot more.'

'Meaning?'

'This marriage will be what you make of it.'

'Haven't you been listening to what I've been saying?' Maxie muttered in confusion. 'It isn't going to *be* a proper marriage, Liz.'

'Right now you are very angry with Angelos. I refuse to credit that you could really go through with walking out on your marriage in six months' time,' Liz told her with a reproving shake of her head.

'I will, Liz...believe me, I *will*—'

'This time I'm definitely not listening,' Liz asserted wryly. 'And as for Angelos's apparent fantasy that he can marry you and live with you on an occasional basis without people finding out that he's involved with you...he's almost as off the wall on this as you are, Maxie!'

'No, he knows exactly what he's doing. He just doesn't expect me to be in his life for very long.'

Liz compressed her lips. 'I have only one real question

107

to ask you. Why can't you just sit down and tell Angelos the whole truth about Leland?'

Taken aback, Maxie protested, 'He didn't want to listen when I did try—'

'You could've made him listen. You are no shrinking violet.'

'Do you seriously think that Angelos is likely to believe that Leland took advantage of me in every way but the *one* in which, of course, everyone thinks he did, even though he didn't?' Maxie was shaken into surprised defensiveness by Liz's attitude.

'Well, your silence on the subject has defined your whole relationship with Angelos. Indeed, I have a very strong suspicion that you don't really *want* him to know the real story.'

'And why on earth would I feel like that?'

'I think that *you* think you're a much more exciting proposition as a bad girl,' Liz admitted reluctantly, and Maxie turned scarlet. 'You get all dolled up in your fancy clothes and you flounce about getting a bitter thrill out of people thinking you're a real hard, grasping little witch—'

Maxie was aghast. 'Liz, *that's*—'

'Let me finish,' the older woman insisted ruefully. 'I believe that that's the way you've learnt to cope with those who have hurt you, not to mention all the mud you've had slung at you. You hide away inside that fancy shell and sometimes you get completely carried away with pretending to be what you're not...so ask yourself—is it any wonder that Angelos doesn't know you the way he should? He's never seen the real you.'

The *real* me, Maxie reflected, cringing where she sat. He would be bored stiff by the real Maxie Kendall, who, horror of horrors, couldn't even read or write properly. And was it really likely that a male as sexually experienced as Angelos would be equally obsessed with possessing a woman who turned out to be just one big pathetic bluff? A woman who had never yet shared a bed with any man? A virgin?

Unaware of the younger woman's hot-cheeked distraction, Liz was made anxious by the lingering silence. 'You're the closest thing to a daughter I'll ever have,' she sighed. 'I just want you to be happy…and I'm afraid that if you keep up this front with Angelos, you'll only end up getting very badly hurt.'

Her eyes prickling, Maxie gave her friend a hug. She blamed herself for being too frank and worrying Liz. From here on in, she decided shamefacedly, she would keep her thoughts and her plans to herself.

Angelos phoned her at six that evening. He talked with the cool detachment of someone handing out instructions to an employee. She knew herself unforgiven. His London lawyer would visit her with the prenuptial contract. The ceremony would take place the following week in the north of England.

'*Next week?*' Maxie exclaimed helplessly.

'I'm organising a special licence.'

'Why do we have to go north?'

'We couldn't marry in London without attracting attention.'

Maxie bit her lower lip painfully. So, Liz innocently assumed that such secrecy couldn't be achieved? She didn't know Angelos. Employing his wealth in tandem with his naturally devious mind, Angelos clearly intended to take every possible precaution.

'Do we travel up together in heavy disguise?'

'We'll travel separately. I'll meet you up there.'

'Oh…' Even facetious comments were squashed by such attention to detail.

'I'm afraid that I won't be seeing you beforehand—'

'Why *not*?' Maxie heard herself demand in disbelief, and then was furious with herself for making such an uncool response.

'Naturally I intend to take some time off. But in order to free that space in a very tight schedule, I'll be flying to Japan later this evening and moving on to Indonesia for the rest of the week.'

'You'll be seriously jet lagged by the time you get back.'

'I'll survive. I suggest you disengage yourself from your contract with the modelling agency—'

'I was on the brink of signing a new one,' Maxie admitted.

'Excellent. Then you can simply tell them that you have changed your mind.'

Maxie was still recovering from Catriona Ferguson's angry incredulity at their brief and unpleasant interview when she was subjected to the visit from Angelos's lawyer.

At her request the older man read out the document she was expected to sign. If Maxie had been as avaricious as Angelos apparently believed, she would've been ecstatic. In return for her discretion she was offered a vast monthly allowance on top of an all-expenses-paid lifestyle, and when the marriage ended she was to receive a quite breathtaking settlement.

By the time he had finished speaking, Maxie's nails were digging into her palms like pincers and she was extremely pale. She signed, but the only thing that gave her the strength to do so was the bitter certainty that in six months' time she would tear up her copy of that agreement and throw the pieces scornfully back at Angelos's feet. Only then would he appreciate that she could neither be bought nor paid off.

The church sat on the edge of a sleepy Yorkshire hamlet. Mid-morning on a weekday, the village had little traffic and even fewer people. Maxie checked her watch for the tenth time. Angelos was *now* eleven minutes late.

Having run out of casual conversation, the elderly rector

and his wife were now uneasily anchored in the far corner of the church porch while Maxie hovered by the door like a pantomime bride, on the watch in terror that the groom had changed his mind. And it *was* possible, wasn't it? The arrangements had been so detached they now seemed almost surreal.

A car had picked her up at a very early hour to ferry her north. And Angelos had phoned only twice over the past week. He would have been better not phoning at all. Her spontaneity vanished the instant she recognised her own instinctive physical response to that rich, dark drawl. It had not made for easy dialogue.

Today, I am getting married. This is my wedding day, she told herself afresh in a daze of disbelief, and of course he would turn up, but he would get a tongue-lashing when he did. Angelos... Hatred was so incredibly enervating, Maxie conceded grimly. He kept her awake at night and he haunted her dreams. That infuriated and threatened her.

In defiance of the suspicion that she was taking part in some illegal covert operation, she was wearing her scarlet dress. A scarlet dress for a scarlet woman. No doubt that would strike Angelos as an extremely appropriate choice.

Hearing the sound of an approaching car, Maxie tensed. A gleaming Mercedes closely followed by a second car pulled up. Angelos emerged from the Mercedes. Sheathed in a wonderfully well-cut navy suit, pale blue tie and white silk shirt, he looked stupendous. As his London lawyer appeared from the second car, Angelos paused to wait for him. As if he had all the time in the world, Maxie noted incredulously. Her ready temper sizzled. How *dared* Angelos keep her waiting and then refuse to hurry himself?

Stepping into full view, her attention all for Angelos as he mounted the shallow steps to the door, Maxie snapped, 'And what sort of a time do you call this? Where the heck have you been?'

As his lawyer froze into shattered stillness, Angelos's

black eyes lit on Maxie like burnished blazing gold. And then a funny thing happened. A sudden scorching smile of raw amusement wiped the disturbing detachment from his savagely handsome features. 'We had to wait thirty minutes for a landing slot at the airport. Short of a parachute jump, there wasn't much I could do about that.'

Suddenly self-conscious, her cheeks flaming, Maxie shrugged. 'OK.'

'Thanks for wearing my favourite outfit. You look spectacular,' Angelos murmured huskily in her ear, before he moved smoothly forward to offer his apologies to the rector for his late arrival.

Minutes later, they were walking down the aisle. As the ceremony began Maxie looked tautly around herself and then down at her empty hands. Not even a flower to hold. And her dress—so inappropriate, so strident against the timeworn simplicity of the church and its quiet atmosphere of loving piety. But then what did love have to do with her agreement with Angelos?

Suddenly she felt the most terrible fraud. Like any other woman, she had had wedding day dreams. Not one of them had included marrying a man who didn't love her. Not one of them had included the absence of her father and of even a single friend or well-wisher. Her eyes prickled with tears. Finding herself all choked up, Maxie blinked rapidly, mortified by her own emotionalism. A ring was slid onto her wedding finger. And then it was over. When Angelos tried to kiss her, she twisted her golden head away and presented him with a cool, damp cheek.

'What's the matter with you?' Angelos demanded as he strode down the steps, one big hand stubbornly enclosing hers in spite of her evasive attempts to ease free of him. 'Why the tears?'

'I feel horribly guilty...we just took vows we didn't mean.'

Maxie climbed into the Mercedes. After a brief exchange

with his lawyer, Angelos swung into the driver's seat and slammed the door. Starting the engine, he drove off. The silence between them screeched louder with every passing minute.

'Tell me, is there the slightest hope of any bridal joy on the horizon?' Angelos finally enquired in a charged and sardonic undertone.

'I don't feel like a bride,' Maxie responded flatly. 'I thought you'd be pleased about that.'

Angelos brought the Mercedes to a sudden halt on the quiet country road. As he snapped free his seat belt Maxie turned to look at him, wondering why he had stopped. With a lack of cool that took her completely by surprise, Angelos pulled her into his powerful arms and sealed his mouth to hers in a hot, hard, punishing kiss. Maxie struck his broad muscular back with balled fists of outrage, but all that pent-up passion he unleashed surged through her like a lightning bolt of retribution.

Her head swam; her heartbeat thundered insanely fast. Her fists uncoiled, her fingers flexed and then rose to knot round the back of his strong neck. She clung. He prised her lips apart and with a ragged groan of need let his tongue delve deep. Excited beyond belief at that intensely sexual assault, Maxie reacted with a whimpering, startled moan of pleasure, and then as abruptly as he had reached for her Angelos released her again, his hard profile taut.

'We haven't got time for this. I don't want to have to hang around at the airport.'

Maxie's swollen mouth tingled. She lowered her head, but as Angelos shifted restlessly on the seat and switched the engine back on she could not help but notice that he was sexually aroused. Her face burning from that intimate awareness, she swiftly averted her attention again. He seemed to get that way very easily, she thought nervously. And only then did Maxie admit to herself that her own lack of sexual experience had now become a source of some anxiety to her.

For a cool, sophisticated male, Angelos had seemed alarmingly close to the edge of his control. If he could react like that to one kiss, what would he be like tonight?

That Greek temperament of his was fiery. Virile, over-whelming masculinity powered his smouldering passion to possess, which she had already frustrated more than once. And, since he believed that she had had other lovers, maybe he wouldn't bother too much with preliminaries. Maybe he would just expect her to be as hot and impatient as he was for satisfaction...

For goodness' sake, Angelos wasn't a clumsy teenager, she told herself in exasperation. As experienced as he un-doubtedly was in the bedroom, he was sure to be a skilled and considerate lover. And he would never guess that she was inexperienced. She had once read on a problem page that most men couldn't even tell whether a woman was a virgin or not.

Honestly, she was being ridiculous! Embarrassed for her-self, Maxie stared stonily out at the passing scenery and forced her mind blank. She smothered a yawn. As the fe-rocious tension drained gradually out of her muscles, tired-ness began to creep in to take its place.

Angelos helped her out of the car at the airport. He frowned down at her pale, stiff face. 'Are you OK?'

'I'm just a bit tired.'

They were flying straight to Greece and they were able to board his private jet immediately. He tucked her into a comfortable seat and, after takeoff, a meal was served. Maxie had about two mouthfuls and a glass of wine. In the middle of the conversation Angelos was endeavouring to open, she noticed that she still had the wedding ring on her finger.

He *is* my husband, Maxie suddenly registered in shock. And then, just as suddenly, she erased that thought. She didn't want to think of him as her husband because she was all too well aware that he did not think of her as his wife. A private arrangement, a temporary one, not a normal marriage, she reminded herself. Her troubled eyes hardened. Sliding the slender band from her finger, she studied it with a slightly curled lip before leaning forward to set it down on the table between them.

'You'd better take that back,' she told him carelessly.

Angelos stared at her as if she had slapped him. A faint arc of colour scored his high cheekbones. His fulminating gaze raked over her. 'You are a ravishingly beautiful woman…but sometimes you drive me clean up the wall!' he admitted grittily. 'Why should you remove that ring now, when we are alone?'

'Because I don't feel comfortable with it.' To evade that hard, assessing scrutiny, Maxie rested her head back and closed her eyes. He was acting as if she had mortally insulted him. But she had no intention of sporting a ring that she would eventually have to take off. On that awareness, she fell asleep.

Angelos shook her awake just after the jet had landed at Athens.

'You've been tremendous company,' he drawled flatly.

Maxie flushed. 'I'm sorry, I was just so tired I crashed.'

'Surprisingly enough, I did get that message.'

They transferred from the jet onto a helicopter for the final leg of their journey to the island. As the unwieldy craft rose into the air and then banked into a turn, providing Maxie with a frighteningly skewed panoramic view of the city far below, her stomach twisted sickly. She focused on the back of the pilot's seat, determined not to betray her fear to Angelos. A long, timeless period of mute suffering followed.

'We're almost there. I want you to see the island as we come in over the bay,' Angelos imparted. His warm breath fanned her cheekbone as the helicopter gave an alarming lurch downward and she flinched. 'Go on...*look*.' Angelos strove to encourage her while she shut her eyes tight and her lips moved as she prayed.

'I totally forgot you were afraid of heights,' he murmured ruefully as he lifted her down onto solid ground again and steadied her with both hands. 'I always come to Chymos in the helicopter. You'll have to get used to it some time.'

All Maxie could think about was how soon she would have to undergo that ordeal again.

'What you need is more of the same,' Angelos announced in a tone of immoveable conviction. 'I have a pilot's licence. I'll take you up in the helicopter every day for longer and longer periods and you'll soon get over your phobia.'

Welded to the spot by such a threat, Maxie gave him an aghast look. 'Is it your mission in life to torture me?'

Angelos dealt her a smouldering appraisal, his hard, sensual mouth curving in consideration while his black eyes glittered over her with what could only be described as all-male anticipation. 'Only with pleasure, in my bed, *pethi mou*.'

CHAPTER EIGHT

WARM colour fingered into Maxie's pale cheeks.

Thirty yards from them a long, low white villa sprawled
in isolated splendour across the promontory. It overlooked
a pale sandy beach, and the rugged cliffs and dark blue sea
supplied a majestic backdrop for Angelos's island home.

'I was born on Chymos. As a child I spent all my va-
cations here. Although I was an only child, I was never
lonely because I had so many cousins. Both my parents
came from large families. Since my father died, this island
has become my retreat from the rest of the world.'
Dropping an indolent and assured arm round her stationary
figure, Angelos guided her towards the villa. 'You're hon-
oured. I have never brought a woman here before, *pethi
mou.*'

As they entered the charming hall she saw into the spacious lounge opposite. In one glance she took in the walls
covered with pictures, the photographs scattered around, the
shelves of books and the comfortable sofas and rugs. It was
full of all the character of a family home. 'It's not like your
apartment at all!' Maxie surprise was unconcealed.

'One of my cousins designed my London apartment. I
did tell her what I wanted but it didn't quite turn out the
way I had imagined it would.' Angelos closed his arms
round her from behind. 'We're alone here. I gave the staff
some time off.'

Maxie tensed. He pressed his wickedly expert mouth to
the smooth skin just below her ear. Every treacherous pulse
jumped in response. Maxie quivered, knees wobbling. With
an earthy chuckle of amusement, Angelos scooped her off

her feet as if she weighed no more than a doll and strode out of the hall down a long tiled corridor.

It was the end of the line of restraint and Maxie knew it. She parted her dry lips nervously. 'Angelos?' she muttered urgently. 'I know you think I've slept with—'

'I do *not* want to hear about the other men who have preceded me,' Angelos interrupted with ruthless precision, glowering down at her in reproof. 'Why do women rush to make intimate revelations and then lie like mad about the number of lovers they've had? Why can't you just keep quiet?'

Not unnaturally silenced by that unexpected attack, Maxie chewed her lower lip uncertainly as he settled her down on the thick carpet in a beautifully furnished bedroom. Her entire attention immediately lodged on the bed.

Seemingly unable to tolerate an instant of physical separation, Angelos encircled her with his arms again and loosed a husky sigh of slumberous pleasure above her head. Curving her quiescent length into glancing contact with his hard, muscular physique, Angelos tugged down the zip on her dress. As cooler air hit her taut shoulder-blades, followed by the sensual heat of Angelos's exploring mouth, Maxie braced herself and surged back into speech.

'Actually,' she confided in an uneven rush, 'all I wanted to say is that I'm really not that experienced!'

'*Theos...*' Angelos ground out, abruptly dropping his arms from her and jerking away to stride across the room. Peeling off his jacket and pitching it aside under her bemused gaze, he sent her a look as dark and threatening as black ice under spinning wheels.

'Sorry, what—?' Maxie began.

'Why are you *doing* this to me?' Angelos demanded rawly as he wrenched at his tie with an exasperated hand. 'Why tell me these foolish lies? Do you think I need to hear them? Do you honestly believe that I could credit such a plea from you for one second?'

Marooned in the centre of the carpet, her dress lurching awkwardly off one bare and extremely taut shoulder, Maxie let her gaze fall from his in a mixture of fierce embarrassment and resentment. If that was his response to the mere admission that she was not a bedroom sophisticate likely to wow him with the unexpected, or possibly even with moves he *did* expect, she could only cringe from the possibility of what an announcement of complete inexperience would arouse. And she did not want to go to bed with an angry man.

'No doubt next you will be offending me beyond belief by referring to the man who kept you for three years...don't *do* it,' Angelos told her in emphatic warning. 'I do not wish to hear one more word about your past. I accept you as you are. I have no choice but to do otherwise.'

Maxie tried to shrug her dress back up her arm.

'And why are you standing there like a child put in the corner? Are you trying to make me feel bad?'

Hot colour burnished her cheeks. 'You're in a very volatile mood—'

'Put it down to frustration...you've done nothing but freeze me out since I married you this morning,' Angelos drawled with raw impatience.

'And you have done nothing but think about sex.'

Having made that counter-accusation, Maxie collided with scorching black eyes of outrage and tilted her chin. Like a child in a corner, was she? How *dare* he? Her bright eyes blazed. The silence thundered. She shrugged her slim shoulders forward and extended her slender arms.

Angelos tensed, eyes narrowing. The scarlet dress shimmied down to Maxie's feet, unveiling her lithe, perfect figure clad in a pair of minuscule white panties and a no more substantial gossamer-fine bra. Angelos looked as if he had stopped breathing. Stepping out of the dress, she slung him a catwalk model's look of immense boredom and, strolling over to the bed, kicked off her shoes and folded herself down on it.

'What are you waiting for? A white flag of surrender?' Maxie enquired drily, pride vindicated by the effect she had achieved.

'Something rather less choreographed, a little warmer and more enthusiastic,' Angelos purred with sudden dangerous cool, strolling over to the side of the bed to stare down at her with slumberous eyes of alarming shrewdness. 'I'm developing a strong suspicion that to date your bedroom forays have been one big yawn, because you really *don't* understand how I feel, do you?'

Face pink, and uneasy now, Maxie levered herself up on one elbow. 'What are you trying to imply?'

'You're about to find out.' Disorientatingly, his bold black eyes flamed with amusement as he began unbuttoning his shirt.

'Is that a threat?' Maxie said breathlessly.

'Is that fear or hope I hear?' With a soft, unbearably sexy laugh, Angelos dispensed with his shirt and gazed down mockingly into very wide blue eyes. 'Your face…the expression is priceless!'

Maxie veiled her scrutiny, her fair complexion reddening.

Angelos strolled across the room, indolent now that he had her exactly where he wanted her, fully in control. 'As for me thinking about sex all the time…don't you know men? I've been celibate for many weeks. I've wanted you for an incredibly long time. I'm not used to waiting and fighting every step of the way for what I want. When you have everything, what you cannot have naturally assumes huge importance—'

'And when you finally get it, I suppose it means next to nothing?' Maxie slotted in tightly.

Angelos elevated a slanting ebony brow. 'Lighten up,' he advised, not even pretending not to comprehend her meaning. 'Only time will decide that. I live in the present and so should you, *pethi mou*.'

He undressed with fluid ease. She watched him. Ever since that night at the cottage, his powerful image had been stamped into her brain like a Technicolor movie still. But she was still hopelessly enthralled, shaken by the extent to which she responded to his intensely physical allure. Yet she had never seen beauty in the male body until he came along. But from his wide brown shoulders, slim hips and long, powerful hair-roughened thighs, Angelos made her mouth run dry, her pulses race and her palms perspire.

'You've been so quiet since that ceremony…and now you recline like a very beautiful stone statue on my bed.' Angelos skimmed off his black briefs in one long, lazy movement. 'If it wasn't so ridiculous, I would think you were scared of me.'

Maxie managed to laugh but her throat was already constricting with nerves. He was so relaxed about his nudity, quite unconcerned that he was hugely aroused. And while common sense was telling her that of course God had fashioned men and women to fit, Maxie just could not begin to imagine *how* at that moment.

Angelos came down on the wide bed beside her. He scanned the sudden defensive upward tilt of her perfect profile, trailed a slow and appreciative hand through the lush tumble of golden strands of hair cascading off the pillows. He threw himself back and closed his hands round her slender forearms to bring her gently down to him. 'And now my reward for waiting,' he breathed with indolent satisfaction. 'Nothing can disturb or part us here.'

Maxie gazed down into smouldering golden eyes full of expectancy. 'Angelos…'

He reached up to run the tip of his tongue erotically along the tremulous line of her generous mouth. 'You feel like ice. I'll melt you,' he promised huskily, deft fingers already engaged in releasing the catch on her bra.

Maxie trembled, feeling her whole body filled with delicious tension. She closed her eyes. He kissed her, and every time he kissed her it got just that little bit more tormenting, and she would open her lips wider, needing more pressure, more passion, begging for it as the floodtide of unstoppable hunger began to build and race through her veins.

He rolled her over and closed a hand over the pouting swell of one pale breast. Her taut body jumped as he smiled brilliantly down into her shaken eyes. 'And yet you are so red-hot, responsive when I touch you. Every time that gives me a high,' Angelos confessed thickly. 'I love seeing you out of control.'

Threatened by that admission, Maxie shifted uneasily. 'I don't like that—'

'You'll have to learn to like it.' Angelos bent his dark, arrogant head over a pink straining nipple and laved that achingly tender tip with his tongue, engulfing her in sensation that she now struggled instinctively to resist.

'No...' she gasped.

'Don't fight what I can make you feel...' he urged hoarsely, employing expert fingers on her sensitive flesh, making her squirm in breathless, whimpering excitement.

Her body wasn't her own any more, but by then she didn't want it to be. With every atom of her being she craved those caresses. Wild sensation was addictive. She was hooked between one second and the next, her mind wiped clean of all thought. The hot wire of his seduction pulled tight as heat flared between her shifting thighs. She moaned his name low in her throat.

He took her mouth with a hot, sexual dominance then. He sealed her to the abrasively masculine angles of his hard, hungry body. She panted for breath when he released her swollen lips, sensually bemused eyes focusing on the brooding intensity of that darkly handsome face now curiously stilled above hers.

'Angelos…?' she mumbled, her fingers rising without her volition to trace the unremittingly harsh compression of his mouth.

He jerked back his head, so that she couldn't touch him. In pained bewilderment Maxie lowered her hand again and stared up at him.

'You used to watch me all the time,' he breathed grimly. 'But the instant I turned in your direction, you looked away…except that once, seven months ago. Then I knew you were mine, as much *mine* as if I had a brand on you!'

Stricken by that assurance slung at her out of the blue, Maxie twisted her head away, feeling naked, exposed. Even then Angelos had been able to see inside her, see below the surface which had dazzled other men. And, worst of all, he had immediately recognised the hunger she had refused to recognise within herself.

'So I waited for you to make your move,' Angelos admitted in a tone of growing condemnation. 'I waited and I waited for you to dump him. But you still stayed *with* him! I began to wonder if you had a single living brain cell inside that gorgeous head!'

He was talking about Leland. Shocked rigid by what he was telling her, Maxie muttered, 'But I…I didn't—'

Angelos vented a harsh, cynical laugh. 'Oh, I know why you stayed with him *now*! You owed him too much money to walk out. Did you think I hadn't worked that out yet? But that's when you reduced yourself to the level of a marketable commodity, and when I think about that it makes me want to smash things! Because, having learnt that wonderful lesson with him, you then sold yourself to me for an even higher price.'

'How *can* you—?'

'What else is this marriage but the price I had to pay for you?'

'You…swine,' Maxie whispered brokenly, white as

death as the contempt he had concealed from her sank into her sensitive flesh like poison.

'And I'll get you out of my system soon if it kills me,' Angelos swore with ragged force as he gazed broodingly down at her.

'Start by letting me out of this bed,' she demanded unevenly.

'No way…I paid with a wedding ring and millions of pounds for this pleasure.'

'No!'

'But you're no good at saying no to me,' Angelos murmured with roughened menace against her tremulous lips. 'Sexually you are one very weak reed where I'm concerned. It's my one and only consolation while I'm making a bloody fool of myself over a woman like you!'

'How dare you?' Maxie gulped.

But Angelos skimmed an assured hand down the taut length of one quivering thigh and kissed her with fierce, angry hunger. And it was like instantaneous combustion. She went up in flames. He didn't hold her down. He didn't pin her to the mattress. He kissed her into submission, tormented her with every erotic trick in his extensive repertoire and the most overpowering physical passion. He swept away her defences with terrifying ease.

Stroking apart her slender thighs, Angelos traced the swollen, moist sensitivity at the very heart of her with knowing fingers. With a strangled moan, Maxie clutched at him in desperation. He controlled her with the hunger she could not deny and made her ache for him. That ache for satisfaction tortured her. He groaned something in Greek, pushing her tumbled hair back off her brow with an unsteady hand, circling her mouth caressingly with his one more time.

As Angelos shifted over her she couldn't get him there fast enough. Her own urgency was as screamingly intense as his. And then she felt him, hot and hard and gloriously male, seeking entrance, and she shivered convulsively, on a high of such anticipation and excitement she was mindless.

So when he thrust hungrily into her willing body she was quite unprepared for the jagged pain of that forceful intrusion. Pain ripped apart the fog of sensual sensation and made her jerk and cry out in shock as she instinctively strove to push him away from her. But Angelos had already stilled to frown down at her with stunned, disbelieving black eyes. 'Maxie—?'

'What are you looking at me like that for?' Maxie whispered in stricken embarrassment, utterly appalled and outraged that her own body could have betrayed her to such an extent.

With a sudden shift of his hips, Angelos withdrew from her again. But he kept on staring down at her in the most mortifying way, his bewilderment blatant. A damp sheen accentuated the tautness of the bronzed skin stretched over his hard cheekbones and the pallor spreading beneath. '*Cristo*…a virgin…' he breathed, not quite levelly.

Maxie lay there, feeling horribly rejected and inadequate and wishing she could vanish.

'And I really hurt you,' Angelos groaned even more raggedly, abruptly levering his weight from her, black eyes holding hers with the same transfixed incredulity with which he might have regarded the sudden descent of an alien spaceship in his bedroom. 'Are you in a lot of pain?'

In one driven movement Maxie rolled off the bed and fled in the direction of the bathroom. Dear heaven, he had been so repulsed he had just abandoned their lovemaking.

'Maxie?' Angelos murmured grimly. 'I think *this* is something we definitely need to talk about—'

Maxie slammed the bathroom door so loudly it rocked on its hinges and then she depressed the lock double-quick. Bang went the image of the cool sophisticate! And without that glossy image she felt naked and exposed. The last thing she could've faced right then was awkward questions. And as she turned on the bath taps she recalled his swinging verbal attack on her before they made love and she burst into gulping tears.

Angelos banged on the door. 'Maxie? Come out of there!'

'Go to hell!' she shouted, cramming her hand to her wobbling mouth before a sob could escape and betray her.

'Are you all right?'

'I'm having a bath, Angelos...not drowning myself! Although with that technique of yours, I understand your concern!'

But no sooner had Maxie hurled those nasty words than she was thoroughly ashamed of herself. He hadn't meant to hurt her, he hadn't known, and lashing out in retaliation because she felt horribly humiliated was unjust and mean. Silence fell. Slowly, miserably, Maxie climbed into the bath.

Only then did it occur to her that it was foolish to be distressed by what Angelos had said in temper earlier. After all, he had now discovered that she could not possibly have been Leland's mistress. So that had to make a difference to the light in which he saw her, *surely*? Only what she had been given with one hand had seemingly been taken with the other. Angelos had been repulsed by her inexperience.

Devastated by that awareness, Maxie thought back seven months to that single exchanged glance with Angelos across that long table in the Petronides boardroom, that charged clash of mutual awareness which seemed to have changed her entire life. Angelos had actually been waiting for her to ditch Leland on his behalf and he had been furious when she hadn't.

Furthermore, Angelos could not now bring himself to speak Leland Coulter's name out loud. In fact he had said she would offend him beyond belief with any reference to Leland before they'd even got into bed. Yet Angelos had been in no way that sensitive to that former relationship when he'd first come to announce his intentions at Liz's house... Men were strange, Maxie decided limply, and none more strange than Angelos.

It took her a long time to emerge from the bathroom, but when she did, wrapped in an over-large short silk robe she had found, the bedroom was empty. It was something of an anticlimax. Maxie got back into bed, not remotely sleepy and very tense, while she waited and waited for Angelos to reappear. A postmortem to end all postmortems now threatened. Having emerged from shock, Angelos would take refuge in anger, she forecast glumly. He would demand to know why she hadn't told him the truth about Leland. He would utterly dismiss any claim that he would never have believed her.

She lay back, steeling herself for recriminations as only Angelos could hurl them. Like deadly weapons which struck a bull's-eye every time. He never missed. And she hadn't been fair to him; she knew now that she hadn't been fair. Liz had been right. She *had* reaped a twisted kind of relish out of pretending to be something she wasn't while she goaded Angelos on and taunted him. And so why had she reacted to him in a way she had never reacted to any other man? Maxie discovered that she was miserable enough without forcing herself to answer that question.

The door opened. She braced herself. Angelos stood poised in the doorway. Barefoot, black hair tousled, strong jawline already darkening with stubble, he looked distinctly unfamiliar in a pair of black tight-fitting jeans, with a black shirt hanging loose and unbuttoned on his bare brown hair-roughened chest.

'I now know *everything*...' he announced in the most peculiar slurred drawl. 'But I am too bloody drunk to fly!'

Maxie sat up. Eyes huge, she watched Angelos collide with the door and glower at it as if it had no business being there in his path. He was drunk all right. And he just looked

so helpless to Maxie at that moment that she abandoned
her stony, defensive aspect. Concern for him took over instead.

Leaping out of bed and crossing the room, she put her
hand on his arm. 'Come and lie down,' she urged.

'Not on that bed.' As he swayed Angelos surveyed the
divan with an extraordinary force of antagonism. 'Right at
this moment I want to burn it.'

Assuming that her vindictive comment on his technique
had struck home with greater force and efficacy than she
could ever have imagined, Maxie paled with guilt but continued to try and ease him in the same direction. Was that
why he had gone off to hit the bottle? Some intrinsically
male sense of sexual failure because he had inadvertently
hurt her? Maxie endeavoured to drag him across the carpet.
He was obstinate as ever.

'Lie down!' she finally launched at him in full-throttle
frustration.

And Angelos *did* lie down. Maxie couldn't believe it but
he sprawled down on the bed as if she had a gun trained
on him. And he looked so utterly miserable. It was true,
she decided in fascination, women were definitely the
stronger sex. Here was the evidence. Disaster had befallen
Angelos when he had least expected it in a field he prided
himself on excelling in and he couldn't handle it.

Crawling onto the bed beside him, Maxie gazed down at
him until her eyes misted over. She was shattered to discover that all she wanted to do was cocoon him in lashings
of TLC.

'You were really great until the last moment,' she told
him in tender consolation. 'I didn't mean what I said. You
mustn't blame yourself—'

'I blame Leland,' Angelos gritted.

In complete confusion, Maxie frowned. 'You blame…
you blame *Leland*?' she stressed, all at seas as to his
meaning.

Angelos growled something in Greek that broke from him with the aggressive force of a hurricane warning.

'English, Angelos…'

'He's a slime-bag!'

Focusing on her properly for the first time, Angelos dug a hand into the pocket of his jeans and withdrew a great wodge of crumpled fax paper.

Maxie took it from him and spread the paper out. It was so long it kept on spreading, across his chest and finally right off the edge of the bed. She squinted down and recognised her own signature right at the very foot. In such dim light, it left her little the wiser as to its content, and in his presence she didn't want to be seen peering to comprehend all that tiny type.

'Leland took advantage of your stupidity—'

'Excuse me?' Maxie cut in, wide-eyed.

'Only a financially *very* naive person would've signed that loan contract,' Angelos extended, after a long pause during which he had visibly struggled to come up with that more diplomatic term. 'And a moneylender from a back-street would've offered more generous terms than that evil old bastard!'

Clarity shone at last for Maxie. Angelos had somehow obtained a copy of the loan agreement she had signed three years earlier. That was what was on the fax paper. 'Where did you get this from?'

'I got it,' Angelos responded flatly.

'Why did you say I was stupid…? Because I'm *not*!'

'You'd still have been paying that loan off ten years from now.' He got technical then, muttering grimly about criminal rates of interest and penalty clauses. She couldn't bring herself to tell him that she had become trapped in such an agreement because she had been too proud to ask someone else to read the small print out and explain the conditions.

'You were only nineteen,' Angelos grated finally. 'You

signed that the day before you moved in with Leland. He
blackmailed you—'

'No…I agreed. There was never any question of us shar-
ing a bedroom or anything like that. All he ever asked for
was the right to show me off. I was just an ego-trip for him
but I didn't know what I was getting into until it was too
late to back out,' Maxie muttered tightly, squashing the fax
paper into a big crunched-up ball again and throwing it
away.

'And Leland was getting his own back on an unfaithful
wife,' Angelos completed grimly.

Unsurprised that he should have known about Jennifer
Coulter's affair, Maxie breathed in deep and decided to
match his frankness. 'My father is a compulsive gambler,
Angelos. He got into trouble with some very tough men
and he couldn't pay up what he owed them. It was nothing
to do with Leland but I went to him for advice, and that's
when he told me he'd loan me the money if I moved in
with him.'

'Lamb to the slaughter,' Angelos groaned, as if he was
in agony. 'Compulsive gambler?' he queried in sudden be-
musement.

'Dad would sell this bed out from under you if he got
the chance.'

'Where have you kept this charming character concealed?'

'I don't know where he is right now. We haven't been
close…well, not since I took on that loan to settle his debts.
Naturally Dad feels bad about that.'

'The debt was *his*?' Angelos bit out wrathfully as that
fact finally sunk in. 'Your precious father stood back and
watched you move in with Leland just so that he could
have his gambling debts paid?'

'It was life or death, Angelos…it *really* was,' Maxie protested. 'He'd already been badly beaten up and he was terrified they would kill him the next time around. Leland

gave me that money when nobody else would have. It saved Dad's life.'

'Dad doesn't sound like he was worth saving—'

'Don't you dare say that about my father!' Maxie censured chokily. 'He brought me up all on his own!'

'Taught you how to go to the pawnshop? Flogged anything he could get his hands on? Your childhood must've been a real blissfest, I *don't* think!'

'He did his best. That's all anyone can do,' Maxie whispered tautly. 'Not everyone is born with your advantages in life. You're rich and selfish. Dad's poor and selfish, but, unfortunately for him, he has too much imagination.'

'So have I...oh, *so* have I. I imagined you,' Angelos confided, his deep dark drawl slurring with intense bitterness. 'The only quality I imagined right was that you *do* need me. But all the rest was my fantasy. Tonight... deservedly...it exploded right in my face.'

Maxie slumped as if he had beaten the stuffing out of her. She wanted to tell him that she *didn't* need him but her throat was so clogged up with tears she couldn't trust herself to speak. A fantasy? He had *imagined* her? That was even worse than being a one-dimensional trophy, she realised in horror. At the end of the day, when fantasy met reality and went bang, there was just nothing left, was there?

'I don't want to sober up,' Angelos admitted morosely. 'The more I find out about you, the worse I feel. I don't like regret or guilt. Some people love to immolate themselves in their mistakes. I don't. How could I have been so bloody stupid?'

'Sex,' Maxie supplied, even more morosely.

Angelos shuddered. It was a very informative reaction.

'Was it that bad?' she couldn't help asking.

'Worse,' Angelos stressed feelingly. 'I felt like a rapist.'

'Silly...just bad luck...life kicking you in the teeth...you get used to it after a while…least, I do,' Maxie mumbled, on the brink of tears again.

'You should be furious with me—'

'No point…you're drunk. I like you better drunk than I like you sober,' she confided helplessly. 'You're more human.'

'*Christos*…when you go for the deathblow, you don't miss, do you?' Unhealthily pale beneath his bronzed skin, Angelos let his tousled head fall heavily back on the pillows. His lashes swept down on his shadowed black eyes. 'So now I know where I stand with you…basement footing—possibly even right down level with the earth's core,' he muttered incomprehensibly.

'Go to sleep,' Maxie urged.

'When one is that far down, one can only go up,' Angelos asserted with dogged resolution.

Well, at least he wasn't talking about flying again. With a helicopter parked thirty yards away that had been a genuine cause for concern. She ought to hate him. She knew she ought to hate him for breaking her heart with such agonising honesty. But the trouble was, she loved him in spite of that two-page list of flaws. She didn't know why she loved him. She just did. And she was in really deep too. He had just rejected her in every possible way and all she wanted to do was cover him up and hug him to death. Flaked out, silenced and vulnerable, Angelos had huge appeal for Maxie.

Why had she spent so long telling herself that she hated this guy? She had been cleverer than she knew, she conceded. Loving him hurt like hell. She felt as if she had lost an entire layer of skin and every inch of her was now tender and wounded. There she had been, naively imagining that he might have been upset because his sexual performance had not resulted in her impressed-to-death ecstasy. And all the time he had been ahead of her, whole streets ahead of her…

The minute he had found out that *he* was her first lover, he had fairly leapt into seeking out what her relationship with Leland had been based on, since it had self-evidently not been based on sex. Naturally he had immediately thought of that loan and probed deeper. And now he knew the whole sorry story and her name had been cleared. But much good it seemed to have done her...

Liz had said Maxie enjoyed pretending to be what she had called a 'bad girl'. Maxie suppressed a humourless laugh. Poor Liz had never allowed for the painful possibility that Angelos, who had exceedingly poor taste in women, was more excited by bad girls than he was by virgins.

CHAPTER NINE

MAXIE wakened the next morning in the warm cocoon of Angelos's arms. It felt like heaven.

Some time during the night he had taken off his shirt. She opened her lips languorously against a bare brown shoulder and let the tip of her tongue gently run over smooth skin. He tasted wonderful. She breathed in the achingly familiar scent of him with heady pleasure. Hot husky male with a slight flavour of soap. She blushed for herself, but the deep, even rise and fall of his broad chest below her encircling arm soothed her sudden tension. He was still out for the count.

And she would probably never lie like this with Angelos again. He was only here now because he had fallen asleep. She had plummeted from the heights of obsessive desirability like a stone. She had lost him but then she had never really had him. He had craved the fantasy, the Ice Queen, not the ordinary woman, and when in so many ways she had played up to that fantasy of his, how could she really blame him for not wanting her any more?

Easing back her arm, she let her palm rest down on that hair-roughened expanse of chest which drew her attention like a magnet. Her fingertips trailed gently through black springy curls, delicately traced a flat male nipple, slid downward over the rippling muscular smoothness of his abdomen, discovering a fascinating little furrow of silky hair that ran...and then she tensed in panic as she recognised the alteration in his breathing pattern. She was waking him up!

And just at that moment Maxie didn't feel strong enough to face Angelos waking up, sober and restored to intimidating normality. Angelos would bounce back from last night's shock and humility like a rubber ball aiming for the moon. Lying absolutely still, she waited until his breathing had evened out again and then, sidling out from under his arm, she slid off the bed.

Gathering up her discarded garments, she crept out into the corridor. Through the open doorway of the bedroom opposite she could see her single suitcase sitting at the foot of the bed. And that sight just underlined Maxie's opinion of her exact marital status. She had *no* status whatsoever. Her possessions belonged in a guest-room because she was supposed to be a casual visitor, not a wife.

Pulling out a white shift dress, fresh lingerie and strappy sandals, Maxie got dressed at speed. It was only seven but the heat was already building. The house was silent. Finding her way into a vast, gleaming kitchen, she helped herself to a glass of pure orange juice and swiped a couple of apples from a lush display of fruit. Determined not to face Angelos until she had sorted herself out, she left the house. Traversing the beautiful gardens, she wandered along the rough path above the beach.

Then she let her thoughts loose, and she winced and she squirmed and she hurt. Their wedding night had been a disaster. And how much of that final confessional dialogue would Angelos recall when he woke up? Would he remember the stupid, soppy way she had hung over him? Would he recognise the pain she had not been able to conceal for what it was? The mere idea that Angelos might guess that she was in love with him was like the threat of death by a thousand cuts for Maxie.

Last night, for the very first time, Angelos hadn't treated her as an equal. Maxie shrank from that lowering awareness. Funny how she hadn't really noticed or even appreciated that Angelos had *always* met her on a level playing field until he suddenly changed tack. Now everything was different. She had been stripped of her tough cookie glossy image and exposed as a pathetic fraud. A virgin rather than a sultry, seductive object of must-have desire. A blackmail victim rather than a calculating gold-digger and the former mistress of an older man.

And who would ever have guessed that Angelos Petronides had a conscience? But, amazingly, he *did*. Angelos had been appalled by what he'd discovered. Even worse, he had pitied her for her less than perfect childhood and her gullible acceptance of that hateful loan agreement. *Pitied*. That acknowledgement was coals of fire on Maxie's head.

Angelos now regretted their strange marriage but he felt guilty. Maxie didn't want his guilt or his pity, and suddenly she saw how she could eradicate both. It would be so simple. All she had to do was tell Angelos about the conditions of Nancy Leeward's last will and testament. When Angelos realised that she had had an ulterior motive in marrying him, he would soon stop feeling sorry for her…at least she would retain her pride that way.

As Maxie rounded a big outcrop of rock, she saw two little boys trying to help a fisherman spread a net on the beach below. As she watched, unseen, their earnest but clumsy efforts brought a warm, generous smile to her lovely face.

'You have never once shown me that ravishing smile.' Maxie was startled into a gasp by the intervention of that soft, rich, dark drawl, and her golden head spun.

Angelos stood several feet away. Clad in elegant chinos and a white polo shirt, he stole the very breath from Maxie's lungs. Her heart crashed violently against her breastbone. He looked drop-dead gorgeous. But her wide eyes instantly veiled. She knew how clever he was. She was terrified he would somehow divine her feelings for him.

'But then possibly I have done nothing to inspire such a reward,' Angelos completed tautly.

He stared at her, black eyes glittering and fiercely intent. In the brilliant sunlight, with her hair shimmering like a veil of gold and the simple white dress a perfect foil for her lithe figure, she was dazzling. Moving forward slowly, as if he was attuned to her pronounced tension, he closed a lean hand over one of hers and began to walk her back along the foreshore.

'From today, from this moment, *everything* will be different between us,' Angelos swore with emphasis.

'Will it be?' Briefly, involuntarily, Maxie stole a glance at him, nervous as a cat on hot bricks.

'You should have told me the truth about Leland the very first day—'

'You wouldn't have believed me...'

His long brown fingers tightened hard on hers. He looked out to sea, strong profile rigid. He released his breath in a sudden driven hiss. 'You're right. I wouldn't have. Nothing short of the physical proof you gave me last night would've convinced me that you weren't the woman I thought you were.'

'At least you're honest,' Maxie muttered tautly.

Apparently enthralled by the view of the single caique anchored out in the bay, Angelos continued to stare out over the bright blue water. 'Considering that there were so many things that didn't add up about you, I can't say that I can pride myself on my unprejudiced outlook...or my judgement. You asked me to stay away from you and I wouldn't. You even left London...'

He was talking as if someone had a knife bared at his throat. Voice low, abrupt, rough, every word clenched with tension and reluctance.

'I have never treated a woman as badly as I have treated you...and in the manner of our marriage I really did surpass myself, *pethi mou*.'

He sounded like a stranger to Maxie. Angelos having a guilt trip. She trailed her fingers free of his, cruel pain slashing at her. It was over. She didn't need to hear these things when she had already lived them, and most of all she did not want *him* feeling sorry for *her*. In fact that humiliation stung like acid on her skin.

'Look, I have something to tell you,' Maxie cut in stiffly.

'Let me speak…do you think this is *easy* for me?' Angelos slung at her in a gritty undertone of accusation. 'Baring my feelings like this?'

'You don't have any feelings for me,' Maxie retorted flatly, her heart sinking inside her, her stomach lurching.

'You seem very sure of that—'

'Get real, Angelos. There are rocks on this beach with more tender emotions than you've got!' Having made that cynical assurance, Maxie walked on doggedly. 'And why should you feel bad for trying to use me when I was planning to use you too? It's not like I'm madly in love with you or anything like that!' She paused to stress that point and vented a shrill laugh for good measure. 'I only married you because it *suited* me to marry you. I needed a husband for six months…'

Against the soft, rushing backdrop of the tide, the silence behind her spread and spread until it seemed to echo in her straining ears.

'What the hell are you talking about?' Angelos finally shattered the seething tension with that harsh demand.

Maxie spun round, facial muscles tight with self-control. 'My godmother's will. She was a wealthy woman but I can't inherit my share of her estate without a marriage licence. All I wanted was access to my own money, not yours.'

Angelos stood there as if he had been cast in granite, black eyes fixed to her with stunning intensity. 'This is a joke…right?'

Maxie shook her golden head in urgent negative. She was so tense she couldn't get breath enough to speak. Angelos was rigid with incredulity and in the stark, drenching sunlight reflecting off the water he seemed extraordinarily pale.

'You do realise that if what you have just told me is true, I am going to want to kill you?' Angelos confided, snatching in a jagged breath of restraint.

'I don't see why,' Maxie returned with determined casualness. 'This marriage wasn't any more real to you than it was to me. It was the only way you could get me into bed.' His hard dark features clenched as if she had struck him but she forced herself onward to the finish. 'And you didn't expect us to last five minutes beyond the onset of your own boredom. So that's why I decided I might as well be frank.'

Turning on her heel, trembling from the effect of that confrontation, Maxie walked blindly off the path and up through the gardens of the house. He wasn't going to be feeling all sorry and superior now, was he? The biter bit, she thought without any satisfaction as she crossed the hall. Now they would split up and she would never see him again...and she would spend the rest of her life being poor and wanting a man she couldn't have and shouldn't even want.

'Maxie...?'

She turned, not having realised in her preoccupation that Angelos was so close behind her. The world tilted as he swept her off her startled feet up into his powerful arms. A look of aggressive resolution in his blazing golden eyes, Angelos murmured grittily, 'It should've occurred to you that I might not be bored yet, *pethi mou*!'

'But—'

The kiss that silenced her lasted all the way down to the bedroom. It was like plunging a finger into an electric socket. Excitement and shock waved through her. He brought her down on the bed. Surfacing, Maxie stammered in complete bewilderment, 'B-but you don't want me any more...you imagined me—'

Engaged in ripping off his clothes over her, Angelos

glowered down at her. 'I didn't *imagine* that clever little brain or that stinging tongue of yours, did I?'

'What are you *doing*?' she gasped.

'What I should have done when I woke up this morning to find you exploring me like a shy little kid...I didn't want to embarrass you.' Angelos focused on her, his sheer incredulity at that decision etched in every line of his savagely attractive features. 'How could I possibly have dreamt that you *could* be embarrassed? Beneath that angelic, perfect face you're as tough as Teflon!'

Maxie was flattered to be called that tough. She didn't mind being told she was clever, or that she had a sharp tongue either. This was respect she was getting. It might not be couched in terms most women would've recognised but she knew Angelos well enough to see that she had risen considerably in his estimation since the previous night. Indeed, it crossed her mind that Angelos responded beautifully to a challenge, and that acknowledgement shone a blinding white light of clarity through her thoughts. She sat there transfixed.

'Why are you so quiet?' Angelos enquired suspiciously. 'I don't trust you quiet.'

Maxie cast him an unwittingly languorous smile over one shoulder. 'I presume we're not heading for a divorce right at this moment...?'

'*Theos*, woman...we only got married yesterday!'

The heat of his hungry gaze sent wild colour flying into her cheeks. He still wanted her. He still seemed to want her every bit as much as he had ever wanted her, she registered in renewed shock. And then he brought his mouth to hers again and her own hunger betrayed her. Her hands flew up to smooth through his hair, curve over his hard jawline. The need to touch, to hold was so powerful it made her eyes sting and filled her with instinctive fear.

'I won't hurt you this time...I promise,' Angelos groaned against her reddened mouth while he eased her out of her dress virtually without her noticing. He cupped her cheekbones to stare down into her sensually bemused eyes, his own gaze a tigerish, slumberous gold. 'To be the first with you…that was an unexpected gift. And telling me crazy stories in an effort to level some imaginary score is pointless. You ache for me too…do you think I don't see that in you with every look, every touch?'

Crazy stories? The will, her godmother's will. Obviously, after a moment of reflection, he hadn't believed her after all. But Maxie couldn't keep that awareness in mind. She did part her lips, meaning to contradict him, but he kissed her again and she clutched at him in the blindness of a passion she could not deny.

'Why should you still fight me?' Angelos purred as he freed her breasts from the restraint of her bra and paused to run wondering dark eyes over her. He brushed appreciative fingers over the engorged tip of one pale breast and then lingered there in a caress that stole the very breath from her quiveringly responsive body. 'Why should you even *want* to fight me?'

There was something Maxie remembered that she needed to tell him, but looking up into those stunning golden eyes she could barely recall what her own name was, never mind open a serious conversation. Angelos angled a blinding megawatt smile of approval down at her and it was as if she had been programmed from birth to seek that endorsement. She reached up and found his lips again, a connection she now instinctively craved more than she had ever craved anything in her life before.

His tongue played with hers as he lay half over her. He smoothed a hand down over her slim hips and eased off the scrap of lace that still shielded her from him. With skilled fingers he skimmed through the golden curls at the apex of her slender thighs and sought the hot, moist centre of her. A whimper of formless sound was torn from Maxie then. Suddenly she was burning all over and she couldn't stay still.

And, as straying shards of sunlight played over the bed, Angelos utilised every ounce of his expertise to fire her to the heights of anguished desire. When she couldn't bear it any more, he slid over her. He watched her with hungry intimacy as he entered her, the fierce restraint he exercised over his own urgency etched in every taut line of his dark, damp features.

The pleasure came to her then, in wave after drugging wave. In the grip of it, she was utterly lost. 'Angelos...' she cried out.

And he stilled, and Maxie gasped in stricken protest, and with an earthy sound of amusement he went on. She didn't want him ever to stop. The slow, tormenting climb to fevered excitement had raised her to such a pitch, she ached for more with every thrust of his possession. And when finally sensation took her in a wild storm of rocketing pleasure, she uttered a startled moan of delight. As the last tiny quiver of glorious fulfilment evaporated she looked up at him with new eyes.

'Wow,' she breathed.

Struggling to catch his breath, Angelos dealt her a very male smile of satisfaction. 'That was the wedding night we should have had.'

Maxie was still pretty much lost in wonder. Wow, she thought again, luxuriating in the strong arms still wrapped around her, the closeness, the feeling of tenderness eating her up alive and threatening to make her eyes overflow. Oh, yes, wouldn't tears really impress him? Blinking rapidly, she swallowed hard on the surge of powerful emotion she was struggling to control.

'I think it's time I made some sort of announcement about this marriage of ours,' Angelos drawled lazily.

Maxie's lashes shot up, eyes stunned at all that went unsaid in that almost careless declaration. Evidently

Angelos no longer saw the slightest need to keep their true relationship a secret from the rest of the world.

'Don't you think?' he prompted softly, and then with a slumberous sigh he released her from his weight and rolled off the bed in one powerfully energetic movement. 'Shower and then breakfast…I don't think I've ever been so hungry in my life!'

Only then did Maxie recall what he had said about 'crazy stories' before they'd made love. Her face tensed, her stomach twisting. 'Angelos…?'

He turned his tousled dark head and he smiled at her again.

Her fingers knotted nervously into a section of sheet. 'What I mentioned earlier…what I said about my godmother's will…that *wasn't* a story, it was the truth.'

Angelos stilled, his smile evaporating like Scotch mist, black eyes suddenly level and alert.

Maxie explained again about the will. She went into great detail on the subject of her godmother's lifelong belief in the importance of marriage, the older woman's angry disapproval when Maxie had moved in with Leland. But Maxie didn't look at Angelos again after that first ten seconds when she had anxiously registered the grim tautening of his dark features.

'You see, at the time…after the way you proposed…I mean, I was angry, and I didn't see why I shouldn't make use of the fact that you were actually offering me exactly what I required to meet that condition of inheritance…' Maxie's voice petered out to a weak, uncertain halt because what had once seemed so clear now seemed so confused inside her own head. And the decision which once had seemed so simple and so clever mysteriously took on another aspect altogether when she attempted to explain it out loud to Angelos.

The silence simmered like a boiling cauldron.

Slowly, hesitantly, Maxie lifted her head and focused on Angelos.

Strong face hard with derision, black eyes scorching slivers of burning gold, he stared back at her. 'You are one devious, calculating little vixen,' he breathed with raw anger. 'When I asked you to marry me, I was honest. Anything *less* than complete honesty would've been beneath me because, unlike you, I have certain principles, certain standards!'

Maxie had turned paper-pale. 'Angelos, I—'

'Shut up...I don't want to hear any more!' he blazed back at her with sizzling contempt. 'I'm thinking of the generous financial settlement you were promised should our marriage end. You had neither need nor any other excuse to plot and plan to collect on some trusting old lady's will as well!'

A great rush of hot tears hit the back of Maxie's aching eyes. Blinking rapidly, she looked away. He was looking at her as if she had just crawled out from under a stone and sudden intense shame engulfed her.

'How could you be so disgustingly greedy?' Angelos launched in fierce condemnation. 'And how could you try to use me when I never once tried to use you?'

'It wasn't like that. You've got it all wrong,' Maxie fumbled in desperation, deeply regretting her own foolish mode of confession on the beach when saving face had been uppermost in her mind. 'It was a spur-of-the-moment idea...I was hurt and furious and I—'

'When a man gives you a wedding ring, he is honouring you, *not* using you!' Angelos gritted between clenched teeth.

Maxie started to bristle then. 'Well, I wouldn't know about that...I only had the supreme honour of wearing that ring for about five minutes—'

'You gave it back—'

Maxie lifted shimmering blue eyes and tilted her chin.

'You *took* it!' she reminded him wrathfully. 'And I don't want it back either…and I don't want you making any announcement to anybody about our marriage…because I wouldn't want anybody to know I was *stupid* enough to marry you!'

'That cuts both ways,' Angelos asserted with chilling bite, temper leashed back as he squared his big shoulders. 'And I'll be sure to ditch you before the six months is up!'

He strode into the bathroom.

Maxie flung herself back against the pillows, rolled over and pummelled them with sheer rage and frustration. Then she went suddenly still, and a great rolling breaker of sobs threatened because just for a little while she had felt close to Angelos and then, like a fairy-tale illusion, that closeness had vanished again…driven away by her own foolish, reckless tongue.

Yes, sooner or later she would naturally have had to tell Angelos about Nancy Leeward's will. But on the beach she had blown it, once and for all. After all, who was it who had told him that she had planned to use him? And the whole thing had struck him as so far-fetched that within minutes of being told he had decided it wasn't true. Indeed he had assumed that she was childishly trying to 'level the score.' Maxie shivered, belatedly appalled by the realisation that Angelos could understand her to that degree…

That was exactly what she had been doing. Believing that their relationship was over, she had been set on saving face and so she had told him about the will in the most offensive possible terms. Now that she had convinced him that she was telling him the truth, she was reaping the reward she had invited…anger, contempt, distaste.

And how could she say now, I wanted to marry you anyway and I needed a good excuse to allow myself to do that and still feel that I was control? There was no way that she could tell Angelos that she loved him. There was no way she could see herself *ever* telling Angelos that she loved him...

When he came out of the bathroom, a towel knotted round his lean brown hips, Maxie studied him miserably. 'Angelos, I was going to tear up that prenuptial contract—'

'You should be writing scripts for Disney!' Angelos countered with cutting disbelief, and strode towards the dressing-room.

'You said...you said you couldn't pride yourself on your judgement where I was concerned,' Maxie persisted tightly, wondering if what she was doing qualified as crawling, terrified that it might be.

'I'm back on track now, believe me.' Angelos sent her an icy look of brooding darkness. 'I'm also off to London for a couple of days. I have some business to take care of.'

Business? What business? They had only arrived yesterday. Maxie wasn't stupid. She got the message. He just didn't want to be with her any more.

'Are you always this unforgiving in personal relationships?' Maxie breathed a little chokily when he had disappeared from view, but she knew he could still hear her.

'I love that breathy little catch in your voice but it's wasted on me. You wouldn't cry if I roasted you over a bonfire!'

'You're right,' Maxie said steadily, hastily wiping the tears dripping down her cheeks with the corner of the sheet.

Angelos reappeared, sheathed in a stupendous silver-grey suit. Lean, dark face impassive, he looked as remote as the Himalayas and even colder.

Maxie made one final desperate attempt to penetrate that armour of judgemental ice. 'I really don't and never did want your money, Angelos,' she whispered with all the sincerity she could muster.

Angelos sent her a hard, gleaming scrutiny, his expressive mouth curling. 'You may not be my conception of a wife but you will make the perfect mistress. In that role you can be every bit as mercenary as you like. You spend my money; I enjoy your perfect body. Randy Greek billionaires understand that sort of realistic exchange best of all. And at least this way we both know where we stand.'

Maxie gazed back at him in total shock. Every scrap of colour drained from her cheeks. But in that moment the battle lines were drawn...if Angelos wanted a mistress rather than a wife, a mistress, Maxie decided fierily, was what he was jolly well going to get!

'Angelos doesn't *know* where you are? You mean he's not aware that you're back in London yet?' Liz breathed in astonishment when the fact penetrated.

Maxie took a deep breath. 'I came straight here from the airport. I'm planning to surprise him,' she said, with more truth than the older woman could ever have guessed.

'Oh...yes, of course.' Liz relaxed again and smiled. 'What a shame business concerns had to interrupt your honeymoon! It must've been something terribly important. When was it you said Angelos left the island?'

'Just a few days ago...' Maxie did not confide that she had left on the ferry exactly twenty-four hours later—the very morning, in fact, when her credit cards had been delivered. Credit cards tellingly made out in her maiden name. The die had been cast there and then. Angelos's goose had been cooked to a cinder.

And, faced with that obvious invitation to spend, spend, spend, as any sensible mistress would at the slightest excuse, Maxie had instantly risen to the challenge. She had flown to Rome and then to Paris. She had had a whale of a time. She had repaired the deficiencies of her wardrobe with the most beautiful designer garments she could find. And if she had seen a pair of shoes or a handbag she liked, she had bought them in every possible colour...

Indeed, she could now have papered entire walls with credit card slips. If Angelos had been following that impressive paper trail of gross extravagance and shameless avarice across Rome and Paris, he would probably still think she was abroad, but he wouldn't know where because she had deliberately used cash to pay for flights and hotel bills.

'Are you happy?' Liz pressed anxiously.

'Incredibly...' Well, about as happy as she could be when it had been six days, fourteen hours and thirty-seven minutes since she had last laid eyes on Angelos, Maxie reflected ruefully. But to vegetate alone, abandoned and neglected on Chymos, would've been even worse.

'Do you think Angelos might come to love you?'

Maxie thought about that. She had set her sights on him loving her but she wasn't sure it was a very realistic goal. Had Angelos ever been in love? It was very possible that she might settle for just being *needed*. Right now, all she could accurately forecast was that Angelos would be in a seething rage because she had left the island without telling him and hadn't made the slightest effort to get in touch.

But then that was what a mistress would do when the man in her life departed without mention of when he would return. A mistress was necessarily a self-sufficient creature. And if Angelos hadn't yet got around to putting in place the arrangements by which he intended to see her and spend time with her, then that was his oversight, not hers. No mistress would tell her billionaire lover when *she* would be available...that was *his* department.

Maxie had tea with Liz and then she called a cab. With the mountain of luggage she had acquired, it was quite a squeeze. She directed the driver to the basement car park of the building Angelos had informed her was to be exclusively hers. She was a little apprehensive about how she was to gain entry. After all, Angelos didn't even know she was back in London yet, and possibly the place would be locked up and deserted.

But on that point she discovered that she had misjudged him. There was a security man in the lift.

'Miss Kendall...?'

'That's me. Would you see to my luggage, please?' Maxie stepped into the lift to be wafted upwards and wondered why the man was gaping at her.

When the doors slid back, she thought she had stopped on the wrong floor. The stark modern decor had been swept away as if it had never been. In growing amazement, Maxie explored the spacious apartment. The whole place had been transformed with antique furniture, wonderful rugs and a traditional and warm colour scheme. King Kong on stilts couldn't have seen over the barriers ringing the roof garden and, just in case she still wasn't about to bring herself to step out into the fresh air, a good third of the space now rejoiced in being a conservatory.

The apartment was gorgeous. No expense had been spared, nothing that might add to her comfort had been overlooked, but, far from being impressed by Angelos's consideration of her likes and dislikes, and even her terror of heights, Maxie was almost reduced to grovelling tears of despair. Angelos had had all this done just so that they could live *apart*. Looked at from that angle, the lengths he had gone to in his efforts to make her content with her solitary lot seemed like a deadly insult and the most crushing of rejections.

Maxie unpacked. That took up what remained of the evening and her wardrobe soon overflowed into the guest-room next door. She took out the two-page list of Angelos's flaws that had become her talisman. Whenever she got angry with him, whenever she missed him, she took it out and reminded herself that while she might not be perfect, he was not perfect either. It was a surprisingly comforting exercise which somehow made her feel closer to him.

How long would it take him to work out where she was? She lay in her sunken bath under bubbles, miserable as sin.

She wanted to phone him but she wouldn't let herself. The perfect mistress did not phone her lover. That would be indiscreet. She put on a diaphanous azure-blue silk night-dress slit to the thigh and curled up on the huge brass bed in the master suite.

The arrival of the lift was too quiet and too far away for her to hear. But she heard the hard footsteps ringing down the corridor. Maxie tensed, anticipation filling her. The bed-room door thrust wide, framing Angelos.

In a black dinner jacket that fitted his broad shoulders like a glove, and narrow black trousers that accentuated the long, long length of his legs, he was breathtakingly hand-some. Her heart went thud…and then *thud* again. His bow tie was missing; the top couple of studs on his white dress shirt were undone to reveal a sliver of vibrant brown skin.

Poised in the doorway, big hands clenched into fists and breathing rapidly as if he had come from somewhere in a heck of a hurry, he ran outraged golden eyes over her re-laxed pose on the brass bed as she reclined back against the heaped-up luxurious pillows as if she hadn't a single care in the world.

'You're here on my first night back…what a lovely sur-prise!' Maxie carolled.

CHAPTER TEN

MOMENTARILY disconcerted by that chirpy greeting, Angelos stilled. His lush black lashes came down and swept up again as if he wasn't quite sure what he was seeing, never mind what he was hearing.

Having learned some very good lessons from him, Maxie took the opportunity to sit forward, shake back her wonderful mane of golden hair and stretch so that not one inch of the remarkably sexy nightdress hugging her lithe curves could possibly escape his notice.

'What do you think?' she asked gaily. 'I bought it in—'

His entire attention was locked on her, darker colour highlighting his taut high cheekbones and the wrathful glitter of incredulity in his brilliant eyes. 'Where the hell have you been for the past week?' he launched at her with thunderous aggression as he strode forward. 'Do you realise that I flew back to Chymos before I realised you'd left the island?'

'Oh, *no*,' Maxie groaned. 'I would've felt awful if I'd known that!'

'Why the blazes didn't you phone me to tell me what you were thinking of doing?' Angelos demanded with raw incredulity. 'You can shop any time you like but you don't need to do it in time that you could be with me!'

'Why didn't you phone me to tell me that you were coming back?' Maxie's eyes were as bright as sapphires. 'You see, I couldn't phone you. None of the villa staff spoke a word of English and I don't have your phone number—'

Angelos froze. 'What do you mean you don't have my number?'

'Well, you're not in the directory and I'm sure your of-

151

fice staff are very careful not to hand out privileged information like that to just anybody—'

'Theos…you're not just anybody!' Angelos blazed, in such a rage he could hardly get the words out. 'I expect to know where you are every minute of the day! And the best I could do was follow your credit card withdrawals as they leapfrogged across Europe!'

What Maxie was hearing now was bliss. She had been missed. 'I think it really would be sensible for you to give me a contact number,' she said gently. 'I'm sorry, but I honestly never realised how possessive you could be—'

'Possessive?' Angelos snatched in a shuddering breath of visible restraint, scorching golden eyes hot as lava. 'I am not possessive. I just wanted to know where you were.'

'Every minute of the day,' Maxie reminded him helplessly. 'Well, how was I to know that when you didn't tell me?'

Angelos drove raking fingers through his luxuriant black hair. 'You do not ever take off anywhere again without telling me where you're going…is that clear?' he growled, withdrawing a gold pen from the inside pocket of his well-cut jacket and striding over to the bedside table.

To her dismay he proceeded to use the blank back page of her list of his flaws to write on. She had left it lying face-down on the table. 'What are you doing?'

'I am listing every number by which I can be reached. Never again will you use the excuse that you couldn't contact me! My portable phone, my confidential line, the apartment, the car phones, and when I'm abroad…'

And he wrote and he wrote and he wrote while Maxie watched in fascination. He had more access numbers than a telecommunications company. It was as if he was drawing up a network for constant communication. Mercifully it had not occurred to him, however, to take a closer look at what he was writing on.

'I got the news that you had reappeared while I was

entertaining a group of Japanese industrialists,' Angelos
supplied grittily. 'I had to sit through the whole blasted
evening before I could get here!'

'If only I'd known,' Maxie sighed, struggling to keep
her tide of happiness in check. Angelos was no longer cold
and remote. He had been challenged by the shocking discovery that she did not sit like an inanimate object stowed
on a shelf when he was absent. He had been frustrated by
not knowing where she was or exactly when or where she
might choose to show up again. As a result, Angelos had
had far more to think about than the argument on which
they had parted on Chymos.

Angelos was still writing. He stopped to sling her a penetrating look of suspicion. 'You were in Rome…you were
in Paris…who were you with?' he demanded darkly.

'I was on my own,' Maxie responded with an injured
look of dignity.

Angelos's intent gaze lingered. A little of his tension
evaporated. Dense lashes screened his eyes. 'I was pretty
angry with you…'

She knew that meant he had been thumping walls and
raising Cain. From the instant he'd found her absent without leave from the island, he had been a volcano smouldering, just longing for the confrontational moment of re-
lease when he could erupt.

'I'd offer you a drink but I'm afraid all the cupboards
are bare,' Maxie remarked.

'Naturally…I wasn't expecting you to move in here.'

Maxie frowned. 'How can you say that when this entire
apartment has obviously been remodelled for my occupa-
tion?'

Setting down his pen, Angelos straightened and settled
gleaming dark eyes on her. 'Look, that was *before* we got
married…you might not have noticed, but things have
changed since then.'

Maxie looked blank. 'Have they?'

Angelos's beautiful mouth compressed hard. 'I've been thinking. You might as well come home with me. I'll stick a notice about our marriage in the paper—'

'No...I like things the way they are.' Saying that was the hardest thing Maxie had ever done, but pride would not allow her to accept the role of wife when it was so grudgingly offered. 'I love this apartment and, like you, I really do appreciate my own space. And there is no point in firing up a media storm about our marriage when it's going to be over in a few months.'

Angelos studied her intently, like a scientist peeling layers off an alien object to penetrate its mysteries. And then, without the slightest warning, his brilliant eyes narrowed and the merest hint of a smile lessened the tension still etched round his mouth. 'OK...fine, no problem. You're being very sensible about this.'

Inside herself, Maxie collapsed like a pricked balloon. He sounded relieved by her decision. He saw no point in them attempting to live as a normal married couple. Evidently he still saw no prospect of them having any kind of a future together. But Maxie wanted him *begging* her to share the same roof. Clearly she had a long way to go if she was to have any hope of achieving that objective.

'But I would appreciate an explanation for your sudden departure from Chymos,' Angelos completed.

Maxie tautened. 'I didn't know when you were coming back. You were furious. It seemed a good idea to let the dust settle.'

'Do you know *why* I came back to London?' Strong face taut, Angelos drew himself up to his full commanding height, the two-page list still clasped in one hand and attracting her covert and anxious attention.

'I haven't a clue.'

'I had to sort out Leland.'

Quite unprepared for that announcement, Maxie gasped. *'Leland?'*

With an absent glance at the loose pages in his hand, Angelos proceeded to fold them and slot them carelessly into the pocket of his jacket. Utterly appalled by that development, and already very much taken back by his reference to Leland Coulter, Maxie watched in sick horror as her defamatory list disappeared from view.

'Leland had to be dealt with. Surely you didn't think I planned to let him get away with what he did to you?' Angelos drawled in a fulminating tone of disbelief. 'He stole a whole chunk of your life and, not content with that, he ripped you off with that loan—'

'Angelos...L-Leland is a sick man—'

'Since he had the bypass op he is well on the road to full recovery,' Angelos contradicted grimly. 'But he's thoroughly ashamed of himself now, and so he should be.'

'You actually confronted him?' Maxie was still reeling in shock.

'*And* in Jennifer's presence. Now that she knows the real story of your dealings with her husband, she's ecstatic. Leland had no plans to confess the truth and his punctured vanity will be his punishment. He trapped you into a demeaning, distressing charade just to hit back at Jennifer!' Angelos concluded harshly.

'I never dreamt you would feel so strongly about it,' Maxie admitted tautly.

'You're mine now,' Angelos countered with indolent cool. 'I look after everything that belongs to me to the very best of my ability.'

'I don't belong to you...I'm just passing through...' Hot, offended colour had betrayingly flushed Maxie's cheeks. She wanted to hit him but, surveying him, she just gritted her teeth because she *knew* that the instant she got that close she would just melt into his arms and draw that dark, arrogant head down to hers. Almost seven days of sensory and emotional deprivation were making her feel incredibly weak.

Poised at the foot of the bed, lean brown hands flexing round the polished brass top rail, Angelos rested slumbrous yet disturbingly intent dark eyes on her beautiful face. 'Leland and Jennifer *do*, however, lead one to reflect on the peculiarity of the games adults play with each other,' he commented levelly. 'What a mistake it can be to underestimate your opponent...'

A slight chill ran down Maxie's backbone. Games? No, surely he couldn't have recognised what she was trying to do, she told herself urgently, for, apart from anything else, she did not consider herself to be playing a game. 'I don't follow...'

'Leland neglected his wife. Jennifer had a silly affair. She wouldn't say sorry. He was too bitter to forgive her. So they spent three years frantically squabbling over the terms of their divorce, enjoying a sort of twisted togetherness and never actually making it into court. Neither one of them allowed for the other's intransigence or stamina.'

'Crazy,' Maxie whispered very low.

'Isn't it just?' Angelos agreed, flicking a glance down at the thin gold watch on his wrist. He released a soft sigh of regret. 'I'd love to stay. However, I did promise to show my face at my cousin Demetrios's twenty-first celebration at a nightclub...and it's getting late.'

Maxie sat there as immobile as a stone dropped in a deep pond and plunged into sudden dreadful suffocating darkness. 'You're...*leaving*?' she breathed, not quite levelly.

'I lead a fairly hectic social life, *pethi mou*. Business, family commitments,' Angelos enumerated lazily. 'But the pressure of time and distance should ensure that the snatched moments we share will be all the more exciting—'

'Snatched moments?' Maxie echoed in a strained and slightly shrill undertone as she slid off the bed in an abrupt movement. 'You think I am planning to sit here and wait for "snatched moments" of your precious time?'

'Maxie...you're beginning to sound just a little like a

wife,' Angelos pointed out with a pained aspect. 'The one thing a mistress must never ever do is nag.'

'*Nag?*' Maxie gasped, ready to grab him by the lapels of his exquisitely tailored dinner jacket and shake him until he rattled like a box of cutlery in a grinding machine.

'Or sulk, or shout or look discontented...' Angelos warmed to his theme with a glimmering smile of satisfaction. 'This is where I expect to come to relax and shrug off the tensions of the day... I'll dine here with you tomorrow night—'

Maxie was seething and ready to cut off her nose to spite her face. 'I'm going out.'

'Maxie...' Angelos shook his imperious dark head in reproof. 'Naturally I expect your entire day to revolve round being available when I want you to be.'

'For snatched moments?' Maxie asserted in outrage. 'What am I supposed to do with myself the rest of the time?'

'Shop,' Angelos delivered with the comforting air of a male dropping news she must be dying to hear. 'Any woman who can spend for an entire week without flagging once is a serious shopaholic.'

Maxie flushed to the roots of her hair, assailed by extreme mortification. She had spent an absolute fortune.

'And if it's a phobia, you should now be very happy,' Angelos continued bracingly. 'With me bankrolling you, you won't ever need to take the cure.'

Maxie was mute. Her every objective, her script, everything she had dreamt up with which to challenge him over the past week now lay in discarded tatters round her feet. As yet she couldn't quite work out how that had happened. Angelos had started out angry, fully meeting her expectations, but he was now in a wonderfully good mood...even though he was about to walk out on her.

During that weak moment of inattention, Angelos reached out to tug her into his arms with maddeningly confident hands. Maxie was rigid, and then she just drooped, drained of fight. He curved her even closer, crushing her up against him with a groan of unconcealed pleasure and sending every nerve in her body haywire with wanton longing.

'If it wasn't for this wretched party, I'd stay...' Angelos pushed against her with knowing eroticism, shamelessly acquainting her with the intensity of his arousal. Maxie's heartbeat went from a race into an all-out sprint. Heat surged between her thighs, leaving her weak with lust.

'I could throw you down on the bed and sate this overpowering ache for fulfilment—'

Maxie said, 'Yes...'

'But it would be wicked and unforgivable to make a snack out of what ought to be a five-course banquet.' Even as he talked Angelos was tracing a passage down her extended throat with his mouth in hot, hungry little forays. He slid a long, powerful thigh between hers to press against the most sensitive spot in her entire shivering body. 'I really do have to go...'

'Kiss me,' Maxie begged.

'Absolutely not...I'd go up in flames,' Angelos groaned with incredulous force, tearing himself back from her with shimmering golden eyes full of frustration.

Maxie clutched the bed to stay upright. Angelos backed away one slow step at a time, like a recovering alcoholic struggling to resist the temptation of a drink. '*Christos*...you're so beautiful, and so totally perfect for me,' he murmured with hoarse satisfaction.

Maxie blinked. All she could focus on was the fact that he was leaving. Everything that mattered to her in the whole world was walking out, and it felt as if it was for ever. The shock of separation from him was so painful it swallowed her alive. And a kind of terror swept over her then, because for the first time she tasted the full extent of her own agonising vulnerability.

She watched him until the last possible moment. She listened to him striding fast down the corridor. She even strained to hear the lift but she couldn't. And then she collapsed in a heap on the soft thick carpet and burst into floods of tears. Dear heaven, what an idiot she had been to set out to provide Angelos with a challenge! All of a sudden she could not credit that she had been so insane as to refuse the chance of making something of their marriage.

He had said that he hadn't expected her to move into this apartment. He had said that she might not have noticed but things had changed. He hadn't even mentioned that wretched argument over that equally wretched will of her godmother's. 'You might as well come home with me,' he had drawled. Her stupid, stupid pride had baulked; he had sounded for all the world like a disgruntled male grudgingly facing up to an inevitable evil. But no matter how half-hearted that offer had seemed, shouldn't she have accepted it?

She would've had something to build on then. Her rightful place as his wife. Instead, she had turned it down, gambled her every hope of happiness on the slender hope that Angelos would learn to love her and want her to be more than a mistress in his life. But, judging by his behaviour in the aftermath of that refusal, she appeared to have offered Angelos exactly what *he* wanted.

No, she had *not* made a mistake in rejecting that offer, she conceded heavily. How long would it have been before he resented the restraints of such a marriage? He had only married her for sex. She shuddered. There had to be a lot more than that on offer before she would risk figuring in the tabloids as the ultimate discarded bimbo yet again.

Angelos certainly wouldn't have been offering a wife snatched moments of his time...nor would he have been taking off for a nightclub on his own. Maxie sobbed her heart out and then, after splashing her swollen face with loads of cold water, she surveyed her weak reflection in the mirror with loathing and climbed into her lonely bed.

Tonight she had got some things wrong, but ultimately she had still made the right decision. She had played right into his hands but it was early days yet, she reminded herself bracingly. Stamina—she needed buckets of stamina to keep up with Angelos. It was so strange, she reflected numbly, every time she rejoiced in the belief that she had got Angelos off balance, he retaliated by doing the exact same thing to *her*...

The instant Maxie was engulfed by the hard heat of a hair-roughened male body, she came awake with a start. Pulling away with a muffled moan of fright, she sat up in a daze. Dawn light was filtering through the curtains.

'I didn't mean to wake you up...' Angelos murmured.

Utterly unconvinced by that plea of innocence, Maxie struggled to focus on him in the dim light. Against the pale bedlinen, he was all intriguing darkness and shadow. Her heart was still palpitating at such a rate, she pressed a hand to her breast and suppressed the lowering suspicion that Angelos might have more stamina than she had. 'What are you d-doing here?' she stammered helplessly.

'It was a long drive home...what do you *think* I'm doing here?' Angelos demanded with sudden disturbing amusement. He rolled over to her side of the bed at the speed of light to haul her back into his arms and seal her into all-pervasive contact with every charged line of his big, powerful frame.

'*Oh...*' Maxie said breathlessly.

'I know anticipation is supposed to be the cutting edge of erotic pleasure but I am not really into self-denial, *agape mou*,' Angelos confided huskily, his warm breath fanning her cheekbone. 'It's been a hell of a week...seven very rough days of wondering if you had left me and found another man.'

As it had genuinely not occurred to her that Angelos might interpret her departure from Chymos in that melodramatic light, Maxie was shaken. 'But—'

'The thought of you out there...*loose*,' Angelos framed with a hoarse edge to his dark, deep drawl.

'What do you mean by..."loose"?'

'The world is full of men like me. If I saw a ravishing beauty like you walking down a street alone, I'd make a move on her like a shot!'

Maxie was not best pleased by that assurance. 'If I ever have the slightest reason to think you're two-timing me, I'll be out of here so fast—'

'How can a husband two-time his wife?'

'He has an affair...*or* a mistress.'

'Well, you've got the market cornered there, haven't you?' Angelos breathed with galling amusement, running his hands down to the curvaceous swell of her hips to cup them and urge her even closer.

Maxie quivered, her body responding with a wanton life all of its own, but she struggled desperately to keep on talking because potential infidelity was an extremely important subject, to be tackled and dealt with on the spot. 'Wh-who was it said that when the mistress becomes the wife, a vacancy is created?'

'Some guy who hadn't had the good fortune to discover you,' Angelos growled with blatant satisfaction. 'You are not like other women.'

Maxie blossomed at what sounded like a true compliment. 'Did you have a good time at the club?'

'What do *you* think?' Angelos nipped at the tender lobe of her ear in sensual punishment and curved her suggestively into contact with the straining evidence of his arousal. 'I've been like this all night, hot and hungry and *aching*—"

Maxie kissed him to shut him up; he was embarrassing her. He seized on that invitation with a fervour that fully

bore out his frustration. She came up for air again, awash
with helpless tenderness. He was irredeemably oversexed
but she just adored him. Something to build on. Obviously
being a sex object was the something to build on. How the
mighty had fallen, she conceded, and then Angelos kissed
her again and all rational thought was suspended...

Maxie crept out of bed and tiptoed across the carpet to the
chair where she could see Angelos's clothing draped. She
would get the list back before he found it. The very last
thing their relationship needed now was the short, sharp
shocking result of Angelos seeing that awful list of all that
she had once thought was wrong with him. That list had
been a *real* hatchet job. After all, when she had written it,
she'd been trying to wean herself off him.

Maxie couldn't believe her eyes when she discovered
that the jacket she was searching *wasn't* his dinner jacket!
Before he had returned to her at dawn, Angelos had evidently gone back to his own apartment to change. She
could've screamed... *Stamina*, she reminded herself, but
her nerves were already shot to hell.

'Maxie...what are you doing?'

Maxie jerked and dropped his jacket as if she had been
burnt. 'Nothing!'

'What time is it?' he queried softly.

'Eight...'

'Come back to bed, *agape mou*.'

Maxie was so relieved he hadn't noticed what she was
doing, she responded with alacrity.

An hour and a half later she sat across the dining-room
table while breakfast was served by Angelos's manservant,
Nikos. He had imported his own staff to remedy the empty
cupboards in the kitchen. His efficiency in sweeping away
such problems just took her breath away. Now he lounged
back, skimming through a pile of newspapers and onto his
third cup of black coffee.

He was a fantastic lover, she thought dreamily. He could be so gentle and then so…so wild. And he ought to be exhausted after only a couple of hours of sleep, but instead Angelos emanated a sizzling aura of pent-up energy this morning. I'm never, ever going to get over him, she thought in sudden panic. I *need* my list back to deprogramme myself from this dependency.

Without warning, Angelos bit out something raw and incredulous in Greek and sprang upright, sending half his coffee flying. Volatile, volcanic, like a grizzly bear, Maxie reminded herself studiously. He strode across the diningroom, swept up the phone, punched out some numbers and raked down the line, 'That piece on Maxie Kendall on the gossip page…who authorised that? You print a retraction tomorrow. And after that she's the invisible woman…you tell that malicious poison-pen artist to find another target. She's supposed to be writing up society stuff, not trawling the gutter for sleaze!'

About thirty seconds later, Angelos replaced the receiver. Maxie was suffering from dropped-jaw syndrome. Only Nikos, evidently inured to the liveliness of life with Angelos, was functioning normally. Having mopped up the split coffee, he had brought a fresh cup, and he now removed himself from the room again with admirable cool.

Angelos slapped the offending newspaper down in front of Maxie. 'This is what happens when you stroll round Paris without protection,' he informed her grimly. 'You didn't even realise you'd been caught on camera, did you?'

'No,' she confided, and swallowed hard, still in shock from that startling knee-jerk demonstration of male protectiveness. She cast a brief glance at the photo. 'But do you really think that newspaper is likely to pay the slightest heed to your objections?'

'I *own* that newspaper,' Angelos breathed flatly, his lean face sardonic. 'And just look at what that stupid columnist has written!'

Maxie obediently bent her head. She put a finger on the lines of italic type to the right of the photo. The tiny words blurred and shifted hopelessly because she couldn't even begin to concentrate with Angelos standing over her as he was.

The silence thundered.

Then a lean brown forefinger came down to shift hers to the section of type *below* the photograph. 'It's that bit, actually,' Angelos informed her, half under his breath.

Maxie turned white, her stomach reacting with a violent lurch. 'I never read this kind of stuff…and you've caught me out. I'm horribly long-sighted…

The silence went on and on and on. She couldn't bring herself to look up to see whether or not he had been fooled by that desperate lie.

In an abrupt movement, Angelos removed the newspaper. 'You shouldn't be looking at that sort of sleazy trash anyway. It's beneath your notice!'

The sick tension, the shattering fear of discovery drained out of Maxie, but it left her limp, perspiration beading her short upper lip. How *could* she tell him? How could she admit a handicap like dyslexia to someone like Angelos? Like many, he might not even believe that the condition really existed; he might think that it was just a fancy name coined to make the not very bright feel better about their academic deficiencies. Over the years Maxie had met a lot of attitudes like that, and had learnt that any attempt to explain the problems she had often resulted in contempt or even greater discomfiture.

'Maxie…' Angelos cleared his throat with rare hesitancy. 'I don't think there's anything wrong with your eyesight, and I don't think it's a good idea at this stage in our relationship to pretend that there is.'

As that strikingly candid admission sank in, appalled humiliation engulfed Maxie. This was her worst nightmare. Angelos had uncovered her secret. She could have borne anybody but him seeing through the lying excuses that came so readily to her lips when her reading or writing skills were challenged. She sat there just staring into space, blocking him out.

'Maxie...I don't like upsetting you but I'm not about to drop the subject.' Angelos bent and hauled the chair around by the arms, with her still sitting in it. 'You are very intelligent so there has to be a good reason why you can't read ten lines in a newspaper with the same ease that I can. And, you see, I remember your notebook when you were waitressing...like a type of shorthand instead of words.'

Maxie parted compressed lips like an automaton. 'I'm dyslexic...OK?'

'OK...do you want some more coffee?' Angelos enquired without skipping a beat as he straightened.

'No, I've had enough...I thought you'd want to drag it all out of me,' she said then accusingly.

'Not right now, if it's upsetting you to this degree,' Angelos returned evenly.

'I'm *not* upset!' Maxie flew upright and stalked across the room in direct contradiction of the statement. 'I just don't like people prying and poking about in what is my business and nobody else's!'

Angelos regarded her in level enquiry. 'Dyslexia is more widespread than perhaps you realise. Demetrios, whose twenty-first I attended last night, is also dyslexic, but he's now in his second year at Oxford. His two younger brothers also have problems. Didn't you get extra tuition at school to help you to cope?'

Relaxing infinitesimally, Maxie folded her arms and shook her head dully. 'I went to about a dozen different schools in all—'

'A dozen?' Angelos interrupted in astonishment.

'Dad and I never stayed in one place for long. He always ended up owing someone money. If it wasn't the landlord it was the local bookie, or some bloke he had laid a bet with and lost…so we would do a flit to pastures new.'

'And then the whole cycle would start again?' Angelos questioned tautly.

'Yes…' Maxie pursued her lips, her throat aching as she evaded his shrewd appraisal. 'I was ten before a teacher decided that there might be an explanation other than stupidity for my difficulties and I was assessed. I was supposed to get extra classes, but before it could be arranged Dad and I moved on again.' She tilted her chin, denying her own agonising self-consciousness on the subject. 'In the next school, after I'd been tested, they just stuck me in the lowest form alongside the rest of the no-hopers.'

Angelos actually winced. 'When did you leave school?'

'As fast as my legs could carry me at sixteen!' Maxie admitted with sudden explosive bitterness. 'As my godmother once said to me, "Maxie, you can't expect to be pretty *and* clever."'

'I don't think I like the sound of her very much.'

'She was trying to be kind but she thought I was as thick as a brick because I was such a slow reader, and my writing was awful and my spelling absolutely stinks!' Feeling the tears coming on, Maxie shot across the room like a scalded cat and fled back to the bedroom.

Angelos came down on the bed beside her.

'And don't you dare try to pretend that you don't see me differently now!' Maxie sobbed furiously.

'You're right. You are incredibly brave to cope with something like that all on your own and still be such a firecracker,' Angelos breathed grittily. 'And if I'd known this when I had Leland in my sights, I'd have torn him limb from limb…because you couldn't *read* that bloody loan contract, could you?'

'Bits of it…I can get by…but it takes me longer to read things. I didn't want to show myself up, so I just signed.'

'Demetrios was fortunate. His problems were recognised

when he was still a child. He got all the help he needed
but you were left to suffer in frustration...you shouldn't
be—you *mustn't* be ashamed of the condition.'

Tugging her back against him, Angelos smoothed her
hair off her damp brow as if he was comforting a distressed
and sensitive child, and she jerked away from him. He persisted. Out of pride, she tried to shrug him off again, but
it was a very half-hearted gesture and recognised as such.
Somehow, when Angelos closed his powerful arms round
her, she discovered, nothing could possibly feel that bad.

'What did that piece in the gossip column say anyway?'
Maxie wiped her eyes on her sleeve.

'That the rumours about you and I were complete non-
sense. But that it looked like you had attracted another
wealthy "friend"—the implication being that he was another married man.'

'The columnist got that bit right.' An involuntary laugh
escaped Maxie.

Angelos's grip tightened. 'It didn't amuse me.'

Maxie then dug up the courage to ask something that had
been puzzling her all night. 'Why aren't you still furious
about me deciding to marry you because of my godmother's will?'

'In your position, I might have reacted the same way. I
fight fire with fire too,' Angelos admitted reflectively. 'I
don't surrender, I get even. But, you see, there comes a
time when that can become a dangerously destructive
habit...'

'I'll stop trying to top everything you do,' Maxie promised tautly.

'I'll stop trying to set you up for a fall,' Angelos swore,
and then he surveyed her with sudden decision. 'And we'll
fly back the island to enjoy some privacy.'

'You really are a fabulous cook,' Angelos commented ap-
preciatively as Maxie closed the empty picnic hamper.

Maxie tried to look modest and failed. In the most un-expected ways, Angelos was a complete pushover. With all those servants around, and the ability to eat every meal at five-star locations if he chose, no woman had ever, it seemed, made the effort to cook for him, and he was wildly and unduly impressed by the domestic touch. If she cracked an egg, he made her feel like Mother Earth.

'You could make some lucky guy a really wonderful wife,' Angelos drawled indolently.

Maxie leant over him and mock-punched him in the ribs. Bronzed even deeper by the sun, narrow hips and long powerful thighs sheathed in a pair of low-slung cut-off jeans, Angelos was all lean, dark, rampantly virile male. She stared down at him, entrapped, heart thumping, breathing constricted. He threaded a lean hand into her tum-bling hair to imprison her in that vulnerable position.

Disturbingly serious black eyes focused on her. 'Tell me, have you *ever* trusted a member of my sex?'

'No,' Maxie admitted uneasily.

'I feel as if I'm on trial. We're married. You won't wear my ring. You still don't want anyone to know you're my wife—'

'You made the offer to announce our marriage out of guilt.'

'I'm not that big a fool. I think you're paying me back for refusing to do it the right way from the start,' Angelos countered steadily. 'I hurt you and I'm sorry, but we have to move on from there.'

Maxie's gaze was strained, wary. 'I'm not ready for that yet.'

'Thanks for that vote of faith.' Releasing her with star-tling abruptness, Angelos sprang upright and strode up the beach.

Fighting a sensation of panic, and the urge to chase after him, Maxie hugged her knees tightly and stared out at the sun-drenched blue of the sea. The first row since they had left London. It totally terrified her. She could not overcome the fear that she was just a fascinating interlude for Angelos, that she did not have what it would take to hold him. She could not face the prospect of being his wife in public and then being dumped a few months down the line when she lost interest...

And yet, to be fair, so far Angelos had not shown the slightest sign of becoming bored with her. In fact, with every passing day Angelos made her feel better about herself, so much more than a beautiful face and body—something no man had ever achieved or even *tried* to achieve.

Yesterday he had had to fly to Athens for the day on business. Three gorgeous bouquets of the white lilies she loved had been flown in during his absence. And every one of them had carried a personal message, carefully block-printed by his own hand. 'Missing you.' 'Missing you more.' 'Missing you even more,' Maxie recalled headily. So impractical, so over-the-top. Not bad for a guy she had believed didn't have a romantic, imaginative, thoughtful, sensitive or tender bone in his entire beautiful body.

But for the past ten days Angelos had been proving just how wrong she had been to attribute such flaws to him. The list? Well, as yet, since that dinner jacket was still in London, she hadn't had a chance to get hold of it, and the list might well have been dumped by Nikos or trashed at the dry-cleaners or some such thing by now. She knew Angelos *couldn't* have found it before they left London. He couldn't possibly have kept his mouth shut on the subject if he had.

He had presented her with a laptop computer with a wonderful spellcheck mechanism on it so that she could write things with ease. He read newspapers with her. He was so patient with her efforts and, as her confidence had risen from absolute rock-bottom inadequacy, she had improved amazingly. How had she ever imagined he was selfish and inconsiderate? And how had she ever thought she could bask in such generosity and not be expected to give something back? And she knew what he wanted back. Total, unconditional surrender. That was what trust was. She was being such a terrible, selfish coward…

Maxie found him in the airy lounge. Hovering in the doorway, she studied him, her heart jumping worse than it did when he took her up in the helicopter most mornings. 'I trust you,' she said tautly, a betraying shimmer brightening her eyes.

Angelos dealt her a pained, unimpressed look, and then he groaned with suppressed savagery. Striding across the room, he pulled her into his arms in one powerful motion. '*Christos*…don't look at me like that, *agape mou*!' he urged ruefully. 'Forget that whole conversation. I'm just not very good at patience…not a lot of practice and too big an ego.'

'I like you the way you are.'

'The lies women tell in certain moods,' Angelos sighed with an ironic look.

'It's *not* a lie, Angelos—'

'Possibly it won't be…some time in the future.' And with that last word he sealed his sensual mouth to hers with a kind of hungry desperation.

The ground beneath Maxie's feet rocked. In that one way Angelos controlled her. He understood that. He used it. She accepted it; the passion he unleashed inside her was more than she could withstand. But, most importantly of all, it was the one time she could show him affection without the fear that she might be revealing how much she loved him. And if anything, after the past ten days, she loved him ten times more.

She was enslaved, utterly, hopelessly enslaved. So the minute Angelos touched her she let all that pent-up emotion loose on him. She clutched, she clung, she heaved ecstatic sighs and she hugged him tight. And he responded with a flattering amount of enthusiasm every time.

Probing her mouth with hot, sexual intimacy, Angelos unclipped her bikini bra. As her breasts spilt full and firm into his palms, he uttered a hungry sound of pleasure. He let his thumbs glance over her urgently sensitive pink nipples. Maxie moaned, her spine arching as he used his mouth to torment those straining buds. She was so excited she couldn't breathe. Reaching down, he unclipped the bikini briefs clasped at her slim hips and pulled them free, leaving her naked.

'I love exciting you,' Angelos confided hoarsely, and he kissed her again, slowly, sensually this time. A long, powerful thigh nudged hers apart. A surge of unbearable heat left her boneless as he bent her back over his supporting arm, splaying his hand across the clenched muscles of her stomach. His skilled fingers skated through the cluster of damp golden curls and into the hot, melting warmth beneath. She whimpered and squirmed under his mouth, and at the exact moment when her legs began to buckle he picked her up with easy strength and carried her down to the bedroom.

He stood over her, unzipping the cut-offs, peeling them off. And then he came down to her. 'Angelos...' she pleaded, aroused beyond bearing.

Answering the powerful need he had awakened, he took her hard and fast, as always disturbingly attuned to the level of her need. And then there was nothing, nothing but him and the wild sensation that controlled her as surely as he did. She cried out as he drove her to a peak of exquisite pleasure and then slumped, absolutely, totally drained.

'Have you ever been in love?' Angelos asked lazily then.

Unprepared for serious conversation, Maxie blinked and met brilliant assessing eyes. 'Yes.'

'What happened?'

Maxie lowered her lashes protectively. 'He didn't love me back...er, what about you?'

'Once...'

Maxie opened her eyes wide. *'And?'*

Angelos focused on her swollen mouth, ebony lashes screening his gaze. 'I fell victim to a feminist with high expectations of the man in her life. She thought I was great in bed but that was kind of it.'

'Tart!' Maxie condemned without hesitation, absolutely outraged to discover he had loved somebody else and, worst of all, somebody wholly undeserving of the honour. There was just so much more to Angelos than his ability to drive her crazy with desire, she thought furiously. He was highly entertaining company and such a wretched tease sometimes...

Dark eyes met hers with disturbing clarity. 'She wasn't and isn't a tart...is that jealousy, I hear?'

'I'm not the jealous type,' Maxie lied, and, snaking free of him with the Ice Queen look she hadn't given him in weeks, she slid off the bed. 'I feel like a shower.'

On the flight back to London, Maxie contemplated the wedding ring now embellishing her finger. It was new, a broad platinum band. It was also accompanied by a gorgeous knuckleduster of sapphires and diamonds.

'An engagement ring?' she had asked him incredulously.

'A *gift*,' Angelos had insisted. But he had produced both at spectacular speed.

Indeed, her finger was now so crowded, a glance at a hundred yards would give the news that she was married to even the most disinterested onlooker. But why couldn't Angelos mention the prospect of having children...or something, *anything* that would make her feel like a really permanent fixture in his life? she wondered ruefully. Maybe he didn't want children. Or maybe he just couldn't contemplate the idea of having children with her. Certainly he hadn't taken a single risk in that department.

They parted at the airport. Angelos headed for the Petronides building and Maxie travelled back to *his* apartment, her new home. Barely stopping to catch her breath, she found the main bedroom, went into the dressing-room and searched through wardrobe after wardrobe of fabulous suits in search of that dinner jacket with her list in the pocket. She found half a dozen dinner jackets, but not one of them contained what she sought. Obviously that list had been dumped. She relaxed.

Angelos called her at lunchtime. 'Something's come up. I may be very late tonight,' he informed her.

Maxie's face fell a mile but her response was upbeat. 'Don't worry, I'll amuse myself—'

'How?' Angelos interrupted instantaneously.

'I'll have an early night.' Maxie worked hard to keep the amusement out of her voice.

'I have this recurring image of you hitting the town on your own.'

'Because you know you got away with going to that nightclub by yourself, but you won't ever again,' Maxie murmured with complete sincerity.

Maxie couldn't believe how much she missed him that night. She thought she would turn over at some stage and find him there in the bed beside her, and it was something of a shock to wake up at eight and discover she was still alone.

By the time she sat down to breakfast, however, the table was rejoicing in a huge bunch of white lilies. 'Missing you too much,' the card complained. Maxie heaved a happy sigh, consoled by the sight. Her portable phone buzzed.

'Thank you for the flowers,' she said, since nobody else but Angelos had her number. 'Where are you?'

'The office. I was out of town last night. It was too late to drive back and I didn't want to wake you up by phoning in the early hours.'

'The next time, phone,' Maxie urged.

'What are you wearing, *agape mou*?' Angelos enquired huskily.

Maxie gave a little shiver and crammed the phone even closer to her ear. The sound of that honeyed drawl just knocked her out. 'Shocking pink…suit…four-inch stilettos,' she whispered hoarsely. 'I can't wait to take them all off.'

'How am I supposed to concentrate when you say things like that?' Angelos demanded in a driven undertone.

'I want you to miss me.'

'I'm missing you…OK?'

'OK…when can I expect a snatched moment?'

'Don't go out anywhere. I'll pick you up at eleven. I've got a surprise for you.'

Maxie flicked through the topmost newspaper and went as usual to the gossip column. She saw the picture of Angelos instantly. Her attention lodged lovingly on how wonderfully photogenic he was, and then her gaze slowly slewed sideways to take in the woman who occupied the photo with him, the woman whose hand he was intimately clasping across a table.

Aghast, she just stared for a full count of ten seconds. Her stomach twisted, her brow dampened. She felt sick. Natalie Cibaud, the movie actress…

CHAPTER ELEVEN

Fresh from reports of an on-off affair with the model Maxie Kendall, Greek tycoon Angelos Petronides, our all-time favourite heartbreaker, seen dining last night with the ravishing actress Natalie Cibaud. Is it off with Maxie and on with Natalie again? Or is this triangle set to run and run?

Last night? Dear heaven, Angelos had been with another woman? With Natalie Cibaud? Maxie just couldn't believe it. She kept on laboriously re-reading the column and staring an anguished hole into the photo. Then her stomach got the better of her. She lost her breakfast in the cloakroom.

Sick and dizzy, she reeled back to the table to study the card she had received with her flowers. 'Missing you *too* much.' There was a certain appalling candour in that admission, wasn't there? Evidently Angelos couldn't be trusted out of her sight for five minutes. And, trusting woman that she was, Angelos had been out of her sight for almost *twenty-four* hours...

Maxie asked Nikos to have the car brought around. She swept up her portable phone. No, she wasn't going to warn Angelos. Nor was she about to sit and wait for him to arrive with whatever surprise his guilty conscience had dreamt up. She would confront him in the Petronides building. Her phone buzzed in the lift. She ignored it.

The phone went again in the limousine. Angelos trying to call her. She switched the phone off with trembling fingers. Offered the car phone some minutes later, she uttered a stringent negative. Getting a little nervous, was he? By now, Angelos would've been tipped off about that piece in the gossip column. He knew he had been caught out. He had been unfaithful to her. He *must* have been. He had been out all night. *All night.* Maxie shivered, gooseflesh pricking her clammy skin. She was in sick shock. Why…*why*? was all she could think.

Until now she hadn't appreciated just how entirely hers Angelos had begun to seem. She had trusted him one hundred per cent. And now she couldn't comprehend how her trust had become so unassailable. He had never mentioned love, never promised to be faithful. On the very brink of making a public announcement of their marriage, Angelos had betrayed her. Why? Was this one of those male sexual ego things women found so incomprehensible? Or was an adulterous fling his revealing reaction to the prospect of fully committing himself to her?

Magnificent in her rage, Maxie stalked into the Petronides building. Every head in the vicinity seemed to turn. They did a double-take at the bodyguards in her wake. Maxie stepped into the executive lift.

Angelos had to be gnashing his teeth. Famous for his discretion in his private life, and his success in keeping his personal affairs out of the gossip columns, he would've assumed he was safe from discovery. Or had he deliberately sought to be found out? Was she becoming paranoid? The simplest explanations were usually the most likely, she reflected wretchedly. Had Angelos just met up with Natalie Cibaud again and suddenly realised that *she* was the woman he really wanted?

The receptionist on the top floor stared and rose slowly to her feet.

Maxie strode on past, the stillness of her pale features dominated by eyes as brilliant as sapphires. Agog faces appeared at doorways. Without breaking her stride, Maxie reached the foot of the corridor and, thrusting wide the door of Angelos's office, she swept in and sent the door slamming shut behind her again.

Angelos was standing in the centre of the room, lean, hard-boned face whip-taut, black eyes shimmering.

A pain as sharp as a knife cut through Maxie. She could read nothing but angry frustration in those startlingly handsome features. That neither shame nor regret could be seen savaged her. 'Before I walk out of your life for ever, I have a few things to say to you—'

Angelos moved forward and spread silencing hands. 'Maxie—'

'Don't you dare interrupt me when I'm shouting at you!' Maxie launched. 'And don't say my name like that. The only way you could get around me at this moment is with a rope! When I saw that photo of you with Natalie Cibaud, I couldn't believe my eyes—'

'Good,' Angelos slotted in fiercely. 'Because you shouldn't have believed what you were seeing. That photo was issued by Natalie's agent *three* months ago! That dinner date took place *three* months ago!'

'I don't believe you,' Maxie breathed jerkily, studying him with stunned intensity.

'Then call my lawyer. I've already been in touch with him. I intend to sue that newspaper.'

Maxie's lashes fluttered. Her legs trembled. She slumped back against the door. Widening blue eyes dazed, she framed raggedly, 'Are you saying that...you *weren't* with Natalie last night?'

'Maxie, I haven't laid eyes on Natalie since the night you took ill. We did not part the best of friends.'

The tremble in Maxie's lower limbs was inexorably spreading right through her entire body. 'But I thought you saw her after that—'

'You thought wrong. I have neither seen nor spoken to her since that night, and as far as I'm aware she's not even in the UK right now. Maxie...you should know I haven't the smallest desire for any other woman while you are in my life,' Angelos swore, anxiously searching her shaken face and then lapsing into roughened Greek as he reached for her and held her so tight and close she couldn't breathe.

'You s-said if you saw a beautiful woman walk down the street—'

'No, I said, "a ravishing beauty like *you*",' Angelos contradicted with strong emphasis. 'And there *is* no other woman like you. When I realised you must've seen that picture, it was like having my own heart ripped out! I can't bear for you to be hurt—not by me, not by anyone, *agape mou.*'

Strongly reassured by that unexpectedly emotional speech, Maxie gazed wordlessly up at him. Angelos breathed in deep and drew back from her. Black eyes meeting her bemused scrutiny, he murmured tautly, 'I have so much I want to say to you...but there is someone waiting to see you and it would be cruel to keep him waiting any longer. Your father is already very nervous of his reception.'

'My...my father?' Maxie whispered shakily. 'He's *here*?'

'I put private detectives on his trail and they contacted me as soon as they found him. I went to see him yesterday. I had planned to bring him back to the apartment to surprise you.' Angelos guided her over to one of the comfortable armchairs and settled her down carefully, seeming to recognise that she was in need of that assistance. 'I'll send him in...'

Stiff with strain, Maxie breathed unevenly, 'Just tell me one thing before you go...has Dad asked you for money?'

'No. No, he hasn't. He's cleaned up his act, Maxie. He's holding down a job and trying to make a decent life for himself.' Angelos shrugged. 'But he would be the first one to admit that he still has to fight the temptation to go back to his old habits.'

Her troubled eyes misted with tears. As Russ Kendall stepped uncertainly through the door through which Angelos had just departed, Maxie slid upright. Her father looked older, his hair greyer, and he had put on weight. He also looked very uncertain of himself.

'I wasn't sure about coming here after what I did,' her father admitted uncomfortably. 'It's very hard for me to face you now. I let you down the whole time I was bringing you up but I let you down worst of all three years ago, when I left you to pay the price for my stupidity.'

Maxie's stiffness gave way. Closing the distance between them, she gave the older man a comforting hug. 'You loved me. I *always* knew that. It made up for a lot,' she told him frankly. 'You did the best you could.'

'I hit rock-bottom when I saw you having to dance to the tune of that old coot, Leland Coulter.' Russ Kendall shook his head with bitter regret. 'There was no way I could avoid facing up to how low I'd sunk and how much I'd dragged you down. I leeched off you, off everyone. All I lived for was the next game, the next bet—'

Maxie drew him up short there. 'Angelos says you've got a job. Tell me about that,' she encouraged.

For the past year he had been working as a salesman for a northern confectionery firm. It was now eighteen months since he had last laid a bet. He still attended weekly meetings with other former gamblers.

Maxie told him that the cottage no longer had a sitting tenant. Her father frowned in surprise, and then slowly he smiled. Rather apprehensively, he then admitted that he had met someone he was hoping to marry. He would sell the cottage and put the proceeds towards buying a house. Myrtle, he explained, had some savings of her own, and it was a matter of pride that he should not bring less to the relationship.

Now he was middle-aged, she registered, her father finally wanted the ordinary things that other people wanted.

Security, self-respect, to be loved, appreciated. And wasn't that exactly what *she* had always wanted for herself? Her father had needed her forgiveness and she had needed to shed her bitter memories. As they talked, her gratitude to Angelos for engineering such a reconciliation steadily increased. Russ had built a new life and she wished him well with her whole heart.

'You've got yourself a good bloke in Angelos,' her father commented with a nod as he took his leave. 'I shouldn't like to cross him, though.'

Maxie was mopping her eyes when Angelos reappeared. She didn't look at him. 'This has been a heck of morning…but I'm really grateful that you found Dad for me. It's like a whole big load of worry has dropped off my shoulders. Tell me, would you have brought us together again if he'd still been down on the skids?'

From the corner of her eye, she saw Angelos still. 'Not immediately,' he confessed honestly. 'I would have tried to get him some help first. But he wouldn't have come if he hadn't sorted himself out. He wouldn't have had the courage to face you.'

Angelos curved a supportive hand round her spine and walked her towards the door. 'We have a helicopter to catch.'

'Where on earth are we going?'

'Surprise…'

'I thought Dad was my surprise.'

'Only part of it.' He urged her up a flight of stairs and they emerged onto the roof, where a helicopter waited. Maxie grimaced and gave him a look of reproach which he pretended not to notice.

He held her hand throughout the flight. Maxie was forced to admit that it wasn't so bad. She was even persuaded to look out of the windows once or twice. But she still closed her eyes and prayed when they started coming in to land.

Angelos restored her to solid ground again with careful hands. 'You're doing really great,' he told her admiringly.

Only then did Maxie open her eyes. She gaped. A hundred yards away stood a very large and imposing nineteenth-century country house surrounded by a gleaming sea of luxury cars. Three other helicopters were parked nearby. 'Where are we? What's going on?'

'I did once mention having a house in the country but you were ill at the time,' Angelos conceded with a wolfish smile. 'Welcome to the wedding reception you never had, Mrs Petronides...'

'I beg your pardon?' Maxie prompted unevenly.

'All my relatives and all my friends are waiting to meet you,' Angelos revealed. 'And the advantage of inviting them for lunch is that they all have to go home before dinner. Two weeks ago, the only reason I agreed to hold fire on announcing our marriage was that I hadn't the *slightest* desire to share you with other people. I wanted you all to myself for a while—'

'*All* your relatives...*all* your friends?'

'Maxie...this little celebration has been in the pipeline for two weeks. The invitations went out while we were in Greece.' He hesitated and cast her a rueful glance. 'I did ask your father to join us but he preferred not to.'

Maxie nodded without surprise and wondered absently why they were dawdling so much on their passage towards the house. 'Was Dad the something that came up yesterday?'

'I went up to Manchester to see him. That took up quite a few hours and then I came back here for the night. I wanted to check everything was ready for us.' Angelos stilled her steps altogether, casting an odd, frustrated glance of expectancy up at the sky.

'What's wrong...?'

The whine of an aircraft approaching brought a smile back to Angelos's impatient dark features. As a low-flying plane approached over the trees, he banded both arms round Maxie and turned her round. 'Look up,' he urged.

Maxie's eyes widened. In the wake of the strange trail of pink smoke left by the plane, words appeared to be forming.

'That's an I,' Angelos informed her helpfully. 'And that's an L and an O and a V—'

'Even I can read letters that big!' Maxie snapped.

The words 'I love you' stood there in the sky, picked out in bright pink. Maxie's jaw dropped.

Somewhat pained by this lack of response, Angelos breathed, 'I wanted you to know that I am proud of my feelings for you...and it was the only way I could think of doing it.'

Never in Maxie's wildest dreams would it have occurred to her that Angelos would do something so public and so deeply uncool. 'You love me?' she whispered weakly.

'You ought to know that by now!' Angelos launched in frustration. 'I've been tying myself in knots for weeks trying to *show* you how much I care!'

Maxie surveyed him with eyes brimming with happiness, but was conscious of a very slight sense of female incomprehension. 'Angelos...couldn't you just *say* the words?'

'You weren't ready to hear them. You had a very low opinion of me...and, let me tell you, few men would've emerged from reading that written character assassination of yours with much in the way of hope!' Angelos asserted with a feeling shudder.

Maxie was aghast. 'You *found* my list—?'

'How could you write all those things about me?'

'There was no name on it, so if you recognised the traits...' Maxie fell silent and studied him with dismayed and sympathetic eyes. 'Oh, Angelos...you kept quiet all this time, and that must've killed you—'

'I used that list as a blueprint for persuading you that I wasn't the man you imagined I was.'

'And you improved so much,' Maxie completed rather tactlessly.

With a helpless groan, Angelos hauled her close and kissed her with devouring passion. Maxie's impressionable heart went crazy. She submitted to being crushed with alacrity and hugged him tight, finally resting her golden head down on his broad shoulder as she struggled to catch her breath again. 'Oh, dear, *I* was the tart who thought you were great in bed and that was all...you were playing games with me when you said that, Angelos!' she condemned.

'That is really rich...coming from a wife who announced she preferred to be a mistress—'

'Only after being told she would be perfect in that role—'

'Perfect wife, perfect mistress, perfect...you are the love of my life,' Angelos confessed rather raggedly. 'Why the hell did I arrange the reception for today?'

Maxie squinted across the sea of big cars at the house. A lot of faces were looking out of the windows. But she didn't squirm. She threw her head high. Angelos *loved* her. The one and only love of his life? She felt ten feet tall. She would never, ever, no matter how long she lived, tell him how utterly naff that pink trail in the sky had been—particularly not when he was so pleased with himself for having come up with the idea.

'I love you too,' she confided as they threaded a passage through the parked cars on their way to the impressive front doors that already stood wide for their entrance. 'I really don't think I ought to tell you, but it wasn't the new improved you that did the trick entirely. I got sort of irrationally attached to you even before I wrote the list.'

'How can you tell me you love me with all these people hovering?' Angelos slung in a gritty hiss of reproach, but he smiled and their eyes met and that devastating smile of his grew even more brilliant.

'I want you to meet my wife,' Angelos announced a few minutes later, with so much pride and pleasure that Maxie felt her eyes prickle.

A whole host of people lined up to greet them. They were mobbed. At one stage it was something of a surprise to find herself looking down on Leland Coulter's balding little head, and then meeting his faded, discomfited blue eyes. 'I'm sorry,' he breathed tightly.

'I made him sorry,' his wife, Jennifer, said very loudly, and Leland flinched and seemed to shrink into himself. 'Everyone knows the whole story now. There's no fool like an old fool.'

The older woman shook hands with brisk efficiency and passed on.

Somewhat paralysed by that encounter, Maxie whispered to Angelos, 'I feel so sorry for him now.'

'Don't you dare…if it hadn't been for Leland, we'd have been together three years sooner!' Angelos responded without pity.

'I couldn't have coped with you at nineteen.'

'I never knew anyone learn to cope with me faster,' Angelos countered, guiding her through the crush to a quiet corner.

Maxie focused on her friend, Liz, in delighted surprise. Petting Bounce, she sat down beside her. 'How did you get here?' she demanded.

'Angelos phoned me last night. We travelled down in a limousine this morning. Bounce was most impressed. Now, didn't I tell you that man loved you? Oh, dear, is he listening?' Liz said with comic dismay.

'Your senses are so much more acute than Maxie's,' Angelos told Liz cheerfully. 'To convince her, I had to hire a plane to spell out "I love you" in the sky.'

'How did that feel?' Liz asked Maxie eagerly.

'It felt…it *felt* absolutely fantastic,' Maxie swore. 'It was so imaginative, so unexpected, so—'

'Naff?' Angelos slotted in tautly.

'No, it was the moment I realised that I loved you most.' And truthfully it had been, when he had unerringly betrayed to her just how hard he found it to put his pride on the line and say those three little words before she said them.

Lunch was a vast buffet served in the ballroom by uniformed waiters. Maxie sipped champagne and drifted about on an ecstatic cloud with Angelos's arm curved possessively round her. She met his aunts and his uncles and his cousins and his second cousins and his third cousins, and all the names just went right over her head.

And then, when the band struck up the music, rising to the role expected of the bridal couple, they circled the floor and the dancing began. Given an excuse to remain constantly within Angelos's hold, Maxie was initially content. Curving herself round him like a vine, she breathed in the hot, familiar scent of his body and inevitably turned weak with longing. 'Any sign of anyone leaving yet?' she kept on asking hopefully.

At last a trickle of departures led to a generalised flood. They saw Liz back out to the limo. Then Maxie and Angelos mounted the stairs hand in hand at a stately pace. 'When did you realise you were in love with me?' she pressed.

'When you had the chickenpox and I still couldn't wait to take you home.'

'But you weren't prepared to admit it—'

'Torture wouldn't have made me confess I was that vulnerable. This is our bedroom.' Angelos cast wide a door with a flourish.

'"Our" has a warm sound,' Maxie savoured. 'I still can't believe you love me...'

'You wouldn't have had to wait so long to find out if you had kept quiet on the beach the morning after I got drunk.' In exasperation Angelos framed her surprised face with loving hands. 'I was ready to tell you. Since I was painfully aware that I had got everything wrong, and I was feeling unusually humble, I was planning to go for the sympathy vote...and what did *you* do?'

'I told you about my godmother's will... I think I'll give my share to Nancy's favourite children's charity.' She stared dizzily into dark eyes blazing with love and gave him a glorious smile. 'I had to tell you about the will some time, but I was just trying to save face. I didn't want you to realise how much I loved you—'

'You're a total dreamer.'

'I'm the love of your life,' Maxie reminded him rather smugly as she flicked loose his tie and slid his jacket down off his broad shoulders with the intent air of one unwrapping a wonderful parcel. 'And you're the love of mine.'

Angelos brought her down on the four-poster bed with a husky laugh of amusement. 'Let me remind you of what you said in your list. Chauvinistic, bad-tempered, selfish, unromantic, insensitive, domineering—'

'A woman always reserves the right to change her mind,' Maxie inserted before he could get really warmed up.

Black eyes were burnished to pure gold as he met her dancing eyes. 'You may be gorgeous...but I think it was your mind I fell in love with...all those snappy replies and sneaky moves, *agape mou*.'

'To think I once thought you were cold.' Maxie ran a tender loving hand over his hair-roughened chest. 'How many children are we going to have?' she asked.

Angelos gave her a startled smile of appreciation that turned her heart over and inside out. 'You want my baby?'

Maxie nodded. The prospect just made her melt.

'You really are tremendous,' Angelos breathed hoarsely.

And then he took her readily parted lips with urgent, speaking hunger and the passion took over, gloriously re-affirming their love for each other.

*   *   *

Ten months later, they had their first child. Maxie gave birth to a baby girl with blue eyes as bright and bossy as her own. Angelos took one look at his daughter and he just adored her too.

Race to the altar—
Maxie, Darcy and Polly are

The HUSBAND Hunters

in a fabulous new
Harlequin Presents® miniseries by

LYNNE GRAHAM

These three women have each been left a share of
their late godmother's estate—but only if they marry
withing a year and remain married for six months....

Maxie's story: **Married to a Mistress**
Harlequin Presents #2001, January 1999

Darcy's story: **The Vengeful Husband**
Harlequin Presents #2007, February 1999

Polly's story: **Contract Baby**
Harlequin Presents #2013, March 1999

Will they get to the altar in time?

Available in January, February and March 1999
wherever Harlequin books are sold.

HARLEQUIN®
Makes any time special ™

Coming Next Month

HARLEQUIN PRESENTS®

THE BEST HAS JUST GOTTEN BETTER!

#2007 THE VENGEFUL HUSBAND Lynne Graham
(The Husband Hunters)
To claim her inheritance and save her home, Darcy needed a husband, *fast!* Her advertisement was answered by Gianluca Raffacani—and while *he* wasn't aware he was her child's father, *she* didn't know he wanted revenge....

#2008 THE SEXIEST MAN ALIVE Sandra Marton
(Valentine)
Finding the Sexiest Man Alive to feature in *Chic* magazine was Susannah's last hope to stop Matt Romano from taking it over. But Matt insisted on assisting her and seducing her. Was he the world's sexiest man...?

#2009 IN BED WITH THE BOSS Susan Napier
Duncan had never forgotten his one night of passion with his secretary, Kalera, even if she had. Now she was engaged to another man...and Duncan vowed to entice her back to *his* bed...for good!

#2010 EXPECTANT MISTRESS Sara Wood
(Expecting!)
Four years after their first brief affair, Adam and Trish were back together again, and she was wondering if this was another fling.... But before she could tell him she was pregnant with his baby, she received a fax from his fiancée....

#2011 ONE BRIDEGROOM REQUIRED! Sharon Kendrick
(Wanted: One Wedding Dress)
Holly had the dress; now she needed a groom! Then she met Luke who was perfect—except that he wanted an *un*consummated marriage! If Holly was to have the perfect wedding *night*, this virgin would have to seduce her husband!

#2012 A FORBIDDEN DESIRE Robyn Donald
(50th Book)
Paul McAlpine found Jacinta mesmerizing, and now they would be spending the whole summer together. But he had to resist her—after all, she was engaged to another man....